Carl Weber's Kingpins:

Jamaica

Carl Weber's Kingpins:

Jamaica

Racquel Williams

www.urbanbooks.net

Urban Books, LLC
300 Farmingdale Road, NY-Route 109
Farmingdale, NY 11735

ISBN 13: 978-1-64556-072-2
ISBN 10: 1-64556-072-4

First Mass Market Printing August 2020
First Trade Paperback Printing December 2018
Printed in the United States of America

10 9 8 7 6 5 4 3 2 1

This is a work of fiction. Any references or similarities to actual events, real people, living or dead, or to real locales are intended to give the novel a sense of reality. Any similarity in other names, characters, places, and incidents is entirely coincidental.

Distributed by Kensington Publishing Corp.
Submit Orders to:
Customer Service
400 Hahn Road
Westminster, MD 21157-4627
Phone: 1-800-733-3000
Fax: 1-800-659-2436

Carl Weber's Kingpins:

Jamaica

Racquel Williams

Dedication

I dedicate this book to my three sons. Over and over, y'all have proven to be the best thing that could've ever happened to me. Each day I get up, I thank Allah for giving me the chance to be in y'all's lives. I love y'all with everything in me.

Acknowledgments

First and foremost, I give all praises to Allah. Without Him, none of this would be possible.

To Nika Michelle, my friend and sister, I want to say a big thank you. God knows I wouldn't have been able to finish this book without your guidance. I will forever be grateful.

And to all my readers and supporters, I love and appreciate y'all. Thanks for rocking with me.

Prologue

Donavan, aka Gaza

"Compound is now open for breakfast," Lieutenant Rodriguez yelled over the loud-speaker.

Fuck. How did I sleep this late? I've waited ten fucking years for this day to come, and my dumb ass fell asleep. I jumped off the top bunk onto the floor. I grabbed my shower bag and rushed toward the shower. To my disappointment, the shower stalls were already packed. Mostly with niggas going to work at Unicor or to the gym for their daily workout routine.

"Damn, homie. This yo' day, ain't it?" my homie Big Cee said to me as we exchanged daps.

"Yeah, you know it, mon. Yo, soon as I touch down, my nigga, I gotcha. You hear me, yo?"

"Man, I already know you got me, bro. Aye, yo, get out there, fuck some bitches, get money, and stay out the motherfucking way. Nigga, I don't want to see you back in here. You heard?" He grabbed me up in a bear-type hug.

"Yo, my nigga, you already know, I'm focused as fuck," I said. "Fuck the Feds. I ain't never coming back to this shit. My nigga, keep yo' head up. You know they passing these laws and shit. Yo' day comin', homie."

"My nigga, I got fifteen bodies on me. Ain't no motherfucking law can get me up out of here unless they drop the motherfucking charges, you dig? All I need you to do is bless a nigga with some change when you send me some pussy pictures. Other than that, go live life, my nigga."

I nodded. "A'ight, man, I got you. I love you, my nigga."

"Yo, lemme go. You know how I hate missing breakfast," he said, trying to hide the tears that were coming down his face. I watched as he ran out of Unit 8H, into the dimly lit federal compound.

I used e'erything in me to fight back tears. Cee was my big homie, my partner up in this bitch. The only nigga that I had confessed a lot of shit to. But he was right; he been down for fifteen years, and the judge had sentenced him to life.

E'erybody knew life in prison meant just that: life. The best I could do for homie to show him how much I appreciated him was to keep his books stocked and send him naked bitches. . . .

"Shower open," a dude yelled, interrupting my thoughts.

"Here I come." I squeezed through, not giving a fuck who was next. I was ready to get the fuck up outta here.

"Nigga, how the fuck you goin' to just cut? You see all these motherfuckers waiting to get in," someone said behind me.

I stopped dead in my tracks, then turned around to face the little pussy nigga that had had the balls to say some shit like this to me. I stepped a little closer to his face. "What the fuck you say to me?" I had my fist balled up. Before he could respond, I hit him dead in his mouth. Before I could get another hit in, I felt someone grab my arm.

"Yo, chill out! You goin' to let a bitch-ass nigga take yo' freedom away?" It was Cee holding on to me.

"Nah, bro. Fuck that nigga. I 'on't give a fuck."

"Man, shut the fuck up. Get in the shower, so you can dress and get the fuck up outta here.

You in a motherfucking position that myself and other niggas would kill to have." I saw the seriousness in Cee's face, and I knew he meant business.

"A'ight, man." I snatched my arm away and walked into the empty stall.

I was still fuming. But I felt where the big homie was coming from. I had a chance to walk out of here a free man today, and here I was, trying to fight. I cut the shower on, releasing the water on my head. I need to get my mind right before I stepped out today. . . .

Twenty minutes later, I was dressed and ready to go.

"Donavan Coley, to R & D. Donavan Coley, report to R & D."

This was my time, I thought as I strutted to the main building. Niggas were passing by me, giving me daps and reminding me to keep in touch. I assured them I would and kept it pushing.

Freedom at last, I thought.

When average prisoners left prison, they'd either go to a halfway house or go straight home if they maxed out. However, for me, it was different, I was on my way to an immigration holding facility, where I would stay until they shipped me back to my home country of Jamaica.

I was ten years old when Mama and I made our way to the "land of opportunities." Those were my mom's words for the United States. Since I was born and raised in the Kingston slum of McGregor Gully, my destiny was already carved out for me. Mama was a higgler who bought and sold clothes, shoes, and whatever else she could get her hands on to support her five children. There wasn't no Daddy, and the few no-good niggas that came around didn't stick around, especially when it was time to come up off that paper.

After watching Mama struggle by herself for a few years, I decided that I had to go out there and get money by any means necessary. I and two of my partners started hustling weed. The business started off slow, but as time went on, it grew. At first, I was able to help Mama with our food bill. Eventually, I was able to afford more. I remembered the smile on my younger siblings' faces when I bought our first television and brought it home. Then I purchased a nice bed, and before you knew it, our little two-bedroom board house was decked out. I smiled as I thought about the joy on my mama's face. . . .

At some point, a relative of ours in the United States offered to help Mama out. So Mama, my oldest sister, and I came to New York one summer, with no intention of going back to Jamaica. The rest of my siblings remained in Jamaica and lived with my grandmother. Mama quickly married some dude and got her green card in no time. About a year later, my sister and I got ours also.

I wasn't no book-smart nigga, not that I didn't know a little something, but my focus wasn't on that. I wanted to make money fast—not a few dollars, but plenty of them. I started off small, with an eight ball, and worked my way up. At first, things moved slowly for me, because I was the new kid on the block. One night at a club in the Bronx, I met two cats from Jamaica, Leroy and Gio. We became a trio and were inseparable. Whether we were grinding or fucking bitches, if you saw one of us, you saw all of us. It didn't take me long to convince them that we could make this money and start running shit. Later, we made friends with a Trini dude, Demari, who would forever change our lives.

It took me about six years to get shit moving the way I wanted it to move. I found a connect out in Cali to supply me with pure, uncut coke. Within a year we were copping twenty-five kilos on each run. Putting in that work, me and my crew of five niggas had the East Coast on lock. We were supplying niggas in Jersey, Delaware, Virginia, and as far away as Florida. Money was flowing in, and so was the hate from other niggas. That didn't stop shit, 'cause after a few altercations and niggas getting dropped, the word was out there that we were not to be fucked with. Shit started getting hot, but that didn't deter me and my crew. Matter of fact, we started going harder at the grind.

I was so caught up in the grind, I was oblivious to the fact that one of my runners, Demari, had got torn off in Delaware by the Feds and had decided to rat on me. What made matters worse was that I had fucked with this nigga hard. Had brought the nigga to my crib, had gone on trips with this nigga, and had even bought this nigga a brand-new Lexus truck. Demari hadn't been moving no way different, so I had had no reason not to trust him or believe he was anything short of loyal.

A year later, I was on my way to one of the trap houses when a black SUV cut me off. I pulled my gun, getting ready to bust at this clown, before I exited my Range Rover. Five other black SUVs pulled up. Niggas jumped out and ran up on me.

"US marshals, get down! Get down!" one of them shouted.

Fuck! I just shook my head. I thought about trying to shoot my way out, but I was surrounded. I looked up and saw a helicopter flying low. It was like in the movies. These motherfuckers were everywhere. They put the cuffs on me, and just like that, my life was changed.

As it turned out, all the trap houses were raided, my niggas were locked up, and accounts were seized. As I sat in my cell in MDC Brooklyn, I kept wondering how the fuck the Feds knew so much about my operation. The answers soon came to me in my motion for discovery. There was an undercover confidential informant. A bitch-ass nigga that I fed had crossed me! My lawyer fought, but in the end, the Feds had too much shit on me. From hours and hours of wiretapping, they had amassed a mountain of information about my drug activities and discussions of shootings. My lawyer advised me to go ahead and plead out.

In the end, the judge sentenced me to 180 months in prison, which was equal to fifteen years. I heard Mama screaming out after the sentence was passed down, but I, on the other hand, was feeling blessed. I wasn't happy, but, shit, with all the evidence that they had on me, they could've easily given me life in prison.

I whispered "I love you" to Mama as the marshal led me away. Within weeks I was shipped to Beckley, West Virginia, to do my time. That had been my home for the past thirteen years. Until today . . .

"Let's go, Reid," a marshal yelled, interrupting my deep thoughts.

I opened my eyes and realized the plane had landed. We were in Rhode Island. This was where the immigration prison was located. Mama had told me that the lawyer said I shouldn't be here for nothing over two weeks. But shit, you know how fucked up the system was; these mother-fuckers did what the fuck they wanted to do. But fuck it. I done did my time. This shit right here was nothing compared to the shit I had done went through in the pen.

As I exited the plane, I stopped and took a long breath. This shit felt good.

"Move it, Coley," this pussy-ass marshal yelled, as if I was his bitch.

I looked at that nigga, smiled as I kept it pushing. In another lifetime, this nigga would never come out his mouth at me like this. I walked off to the van that they had waiting. We all climbed in and sat there waiting in the hot-ass van, laughing and talking.

"Yo, it's fucking hot in here," a nigga in the back hollered.

But his plea fell on deaf ears. The marshals continued on about their business, ignoring us.

"Yo, pussy. It's hot up in dis van," I yelled.

"What the fuck you just said?" said a white, redneck, bitch-ass nigga as he stepped in the van.

"Nigga, you heard what the fuck I said." I looked that nigga dead in the face. We stared each other down for a good two minutes. This nigga finally backed away. I knew he'd seen in my eyes that there wasn't no bitch in my blood.

Minutes later the other bitch-ass nigga got in the van and pulled off. About thirty minutes later, we arrived at the immigration prison, climbed out of the van, and marched inside. I was eager to get in there, to get a shower, and get something to eat. This small prison was nothing compared to the one I had come from. It was quiet, and I welcomed that. After being in the pen all those years and being around niggas, being in a quieter place was far better. Once you got in bed in the pen, you could never really get a good night's sleep, because niggas were constantly getting killed. You had to be on guard all the time, or you might just be the next victim.

Being the nigga I was, I was always on guard, 'cause I had promised Mama that I would come home to her alive, and not in a body bag, and that was a promise that I could not break. . . .

Chapter One

Gaza

It was surprising how shit had changed in the thirteen years that I'd been gone. I had left Jamaica with Mama and my sister at the age of twenty-two, and here I was, returning at thirty-five, a grown-ass man. I felt kind of funny as I stepped off the United Airlines flight that had taken me from Rhode Island to Kingston, Jamaica. Yes, I was born at Jubilee Hospital and raised in McGregor Gully. When you mentioned the Gully, niggas automatically knew what you were all about. If you were from the Gully, you already knew we were all 'bout our paper. Either we were slinging them rocks, sticking up other dope boys, or pimping bitches out. We were goin' to get it one way or the other. . . .

It was humid as fuck, but it felt good. I stood outside, inhaling and exhaling the air on this hot August day. I looked around me; nothing seemed familiar. The last time I was here, in my country, I was a little-ass young man. I ain't goin' to lie: I started feeling crazy as fuck. I felt everyone was staring at me. I knew they were aware that this was the plane that carried the deportees.

After going through customs, I finally walked out the door. People were everywhere, and cars were pulling up to the curb. I felt like I wanted to run back inside the terminal, hide from all this chaos around me. . . .

"Donavan." I heard someone yellin' my government. I immediately recognized the voice without seeing the face.

I looked at the crowd of people that were standing around, and there was my mama, my queen, waving at me. I smiled and pushed through the crowd, trying to get to her.

"Oh my God. My baby is free!" she screamed as she hugged me. Then she started planting kisses on my forehead.

Seconds later a car pulled up, and dude started honking his horn at us.

"Go the fuck around. You see me hugging ma child," Mama said and flicked the man a bird.

"Come on, Mama. 'Cause if him, that pussy, say anything to you, it's gonna be bloodshed out here today." I was so serious, and I let it be known.

She finally let me go out of her tight embrace, pointed to her car, and climbed behind the wheel. I threw the envelopes that I had in my possession on the backseat and then got in the front passenger seat. Mama pulled off, still cussing the man out with her raw Jamaican accent, which seemed to get stronger the older she got.

"Damn, Ma. Ain't nothing change. You still a gangsta," I joked.

"Baby, don't yuh start, now. You know yuh mama can handle herself."

Her ass was nothing but about four feet five, but you couldn't tell by her voice, which was strong whenever she spoke. Mama was the type to whup on niggas and bitches. I remembered how she used to beat this nigga Tony that she used to fuck with back when we lived in Jamaica. I mean, Mama used to use a broomstick on that nigga. It was funny as hell, because this nigga was big and bulky. He used to run out of the house, yelling cusswords until he got outside the gate. Thinking back on those good old days, I couldn't help bursting into laughter.

"What the hell so funny, boy?"

"Ma, you remember how you used to run after Tony, hitting him with a broomstick and shit?"

"That damn fool Tony. You know he got killed a few years back? Gunmen ran up in his house in Portmore and killed him and his son. Word had it, him and his son was wrapped up in that scamming thing."

"Really? That's fucked up."

"Boy, watch yo' damn mout'," she said with her raw Jamaican accent.

"My bad, Mama, but you do know I'm thirty-five years old now, right?"

She swung that neck around so fast and looked at me. "And what's that supposed to mean?"

"Just easy yo' self. You done know how do things set already."

"Uh-huh. So how it feel to be among the free?"

"You know, I don't really feel it as yet. Ask mi dis same question in about a month."

"Well, I'm just happy you are here. I pray night and day fi God to let you come home to me safe and sound. And here you are, my baby," she said.

"You done know mi a God bless and Father God not leaving my side."

"Well, everybody is at the house, waiting fa you. They are so happy you home."

"Oh yeah." I smiled.

It had been thirteen years since I'd seen my family. As I said, my mom, my oldest sister, and I were the only ones that had made it to the United States. The rest of my family had stayed in Jamaica, with my grandmother. I was really excited just to be in the presence of people that I knew genuinely loved me. . . .

I watched as Mama pulled up at a gate outside the three-story crib that my money had helped build after we left Jamaica. This was one of the first things I had done when I started making money in New York. I was as proud of it as I was of the big house in New York that I had bought Mama. When the Feds had got me, they couldn't touch neither house, 'cause Mama worked, had money in the bank, and had the houses in her name, and they couldn't prove she knew anything about my illegal activities. My mama wasn't no fool, and she handled her shit like a real G.

"Oh shit! This is it, Mama?" I said as she punched the code in the keypad. She waited for the gate to open and then drove up the marble driveway.

"Yes, son, this is it," she answered as the gate swung shut behind us.

After she stopped the car and turned off the ignition, I stepped out of the car and just stood there, looking. This house was more beautiful in person than it was in the pictures I had seen.

"Gaza is here," I heard one of brothers yell.

All I saw out of the corner of my eye was people rushing out of the house. Not just any people, though. Familiar faces ran up to me and almost knocked me to the ground.

"What's good, family?" said the same brother who had announced my arrival. He hugged me tight. See, this was the brother that I was closest to, and he was the one that everybody said was my twin. We hugged for a good minute before my grandma interrupted.

"Mi grandbaby. Come give yo' grandmother a big hug." She pushed my brother out of the way.

"Grandma Rosie, what a gwaan?" I tried to use my rawest patois on her.

"Welcome home, mi baby. Come. I know you must hungry." She took my hand and led me into the house. That didn't stop everyone else from following behind us. The treatment that I was getting was nothing short of that afforded royalty.

My grandma ushered me into the dining room. On the long table were large bowls of curry goat, white rice, oxtails, and jerk chicken, as well as a big jar of sorrel punch. Wait, it wasn't even Christmastime, and sorrel was being served. I smiled as I looked at the family members surrounding me. This was the place I need to be, among real family. . . .

It was a little after 11:00 p.m., and all the festivities had died down. I kissed Grandma on the cheek after she gave me a very serious tongue-lashing about my troubles with the law. I guessed this was long overdue.

I walked out on the balcony, with a Guinness in hand, and rolled me a blunt. I welcomed this serene feeling I was experiencing right now. I took a long drag of the weed and instantly started to choke. I mean, a nigga ain't smoked in a few years. When I first got to the pen, me and one of my cellies used to hustle the weed inside. But just as on the outside, niggas started snitching. After my cellie got caught and more time was added to the twenty years he was doing, I decided to chill out. My black ass was trying to come up out of there, not add a single day to what that bitch-ass judge had done gave me.

The house was up in the hills of Cherry Gardens and overlooked the entire downtown. The view was spectacular to a nigga that had had to look at brick buildings for over a decade. I sipped on the Guinness, took a few more pulls, being careful not to choke.

"Yo, Father, what's the pree?" said a male voice behind me.

"Oh shit! My nigga," I exclaimed as I turned around.

It was my right-hand man, Gio. He was my partner from back in the day, had run with me in New York.

"Yo, Father, how freedom feel?"

"Feel motherfucking good. This is what I been waitin' on." I looked around, inhaling the fresh Jamaican air.

"Welcome home, nigga." He gave me dap; then he handed me a key fob and a cell phone.

"What's this, yo?" I shot him a suspicious look.

"Go out front and see fa yourself."

He walked back inside the house, made his way to the foyer, went out the front door, and headed down the steps to the driveway. I followed him. Outside of the crib sat a black BMW with rims. I walked over to it and stared at the beauty.

"This is your ride. Welcome home, Father," Gio said.

I looked at him to see if this was a big joke, but he stood there, with a serious look plastered all over his face. I looked down at the key fob in my hand, didn't see a key. "Yo, where's the key?"

"Oh shit. I forgot you been gone for a minute. This a keyless, push-button car. Yo, we don't drive vehicles if they not push button. Press the button on the fob and open it up."

This was dope as shit. I looked down at the key fob, pressed the UNLOCK button. I then opened the car door, climbed in, and pressed the START button. Nothing. "Yo, what the hell? Why it ain't starting?"

He leaned in the car. "Put yo' foot 'pon the brake pedal."

He then pushed the button. The car started. Yo, this was new to me. I hadn't driven in years, but I was eager to test out my new whip.

"Hop in, nigga," I told him.

He jumped in on the passenger side, and I pulled off. The ride started off a little rough, 'cause this baby had power and a nigga was rusty, but I quickly got it under control. I went around the block a few times, catching the stares of bitches and niggas that were hanging out late. Then we went back to the house, and we drank a bottle of Patrón that he had brought over and smoked blunts back-to-back on the balcony. It felt good to have in my presence one of my niggas who had been rolling with me from day one. It was a little after 5:00 a.m. when he rolled out and I left the balcony and went back into the house. I took a quick shower before going into my bedroom. It felt so good to be in a real bed, and not on that cot they had in jail. Before I knew it, a nigga was out. . . .

I heard banging on the bedroom door, which woke me up out of my sleep. I jumped up, looked around. That was when I realized I wasn't in prison. I had been in a deep sleep when the knocking startled me. . . .

"Donavan, you still sleeping?" Mama's voice echoed through the crack in the door.

Oh shit. I had forgotten she was leaving, was going back to the States today. I was supposed to take her to the airport. I grabbed my phone and looked at the time. It was well after 12:00 p.m. "I'm up, Mama. Give me a few minutes."

I rushed to the bathroom, took a quick shower, and grabbed one of the white T-shirts and jean shorts Mama had brought down for me. In no time, I was dressed and ready to go. I walked in the kitchen, where my grandma was sitting with an older-looking woman.

"Doris, this is the man of the house, Donavan. He will be your new boss."

Doris stood, walked over to me, and shook my hand. "Nice to meet you, young man. I hear all good things 'bout you."

"Nice to meet you too, Miss Doris."

My mother walked in just then. "Your breakfast is on the dining-room table," she said.

"Thanks, Mama, but I'm ready to take you to the airport."

"Donavon, is who car parked out in the front?" my mother asked.

"It's mine, Mama."

"Is yours?" She stopped dead in her tracks, turned around, and looked at me.

That lady's look had never changed over the years. Whenever she was displeased with any one of us, she had a special look that she would shoot our way. This time was no different, but the only thing was, I was no longer a little boy and I wasn't afraid to face her.

"You late, right? You 'on't wanna miss that flight," I reminded her.

I left the kitchen, grabbed her bags in the foyer, carried them out, and then placed them in the trunk of the car. I got behind the wheel and waited for her. She finally appeared and got in the passenger seat, and then we drove off. I could tell she was feeling some type of way, 'cause her mood had changed drastically.

"Donavan . . . I know you're grown and I can't tell you how to live ya life, but Jamaica is not a nice place. You left here when you was a young man. Now it's more killing. Don't come down here and get wrap up with these bwoy down here."

"Mama, listen, you need to stop worrying. I'm good, trust me."

"You betta be, 'cause I don't want to lose you. Don't you trust none of these people down yah. You been gone too damn long to come down yah and lose your life."

"Mama, come on. You worry too much, mon. Relax. I want you fi go home and focus on enjoying life. Trust me, I got this."

"All right. Me warning you. My mother always say, 'A hard head make a soft ass.'"

I burst out laughing. "Mama, you have always said the same thing too."

She didn't respond; instead, she turned her head and stared out the window. I cut on the music to kind of mellow out the mood.

When we reached the airport, I pulled over to the curb and unloaded Mama's luggage. When she got out of the car, I turned to her and said, "I love you, Mama." I hugged her tight as she professed her love for me and repeated that these people were no good.

Then I watched as she strutted into the airport terminal. When she looked back, I waved one last time. After she had disappeared inside the terminal, I hopped back in the car and pulled off.

Chapter Two

Gaza

Six months later . . .

Pop! Pop! Pop!

Gunshots rang out at Club Mirage, one of the most popular nightclubs in Kingston. I grabbed my gun as I ducked by the side of the table where me and a few niggas had been drinking liquor and vibing.

"Yo, what the fuck is that?" I said.

"Yo, some niggas up front a shoot in a di place," my partner Gio answered.

"This the shit I'm talkin' 'bout. This why I don't like to be round niggas like that," I muttered. "Now the fucking police goin' to definitely come through."

"Yo, let's get out of here," Gio urged. "I know the back way."

"A'ight, bet."

We all got up and made our way to the back entrance. I guessed we were not the only ones aware of it, 'cause bitches and niggas were making their way out the door also. Soon as we got outside, multiple police cars were pulling up.

I dashed to my car, jumped in, and sped off, wanting to get far away from the chaos that was taking place back there. My phone started ringing. It was my nigga.

"Yo."

"Man, I hear it's the nigga Yellow Man from Grants Pen that got killed tonight."

"Yellow Man? I don't remember him, but damn, that's fucked up, B. These niggas making the spot hot as fuck. I'm glad we got the fuck up outta there, yo."

"Yeah, yo, anyways, I'ma head to this catty house on Waltham. Link you in the a.m."

"A'ight, yo."

Shit. It was late, and after all that had happened tonight, I guessed I was going to call it a night. I got some shit to do in the morning, and I needed a fresh mind in order to execute these plans.

Being back in Jamaica was cool and everything. I had been trying to stay out the spotlight because it had been years since I lived here. But shit was getting hectic now; money was getting tight. I had started out fucking with the ganja, but truthfully, there wasn't no big money in it. It was just chump change compared to what I was used to making. So it was time to put some big plan into motion, and I already got some niggas in mind.

After eating some breakfast, I decided to meet up with my big homie Gio around the way. I'd hadn't been to McGregor Gully since I got back to Jamaica. But my niggas still frequented the area and had a stronghold on everything that went on around there. So that was where I was headed today.

I jumped in my car and headed out. Money was on my mind, and there was nothing or no one that was going to stand in the way of that. I was a boss that was used to four or five cars at a time, multiple houses in different cities. This poor shit, living dollar to dollar or depending on Mom Dukes to send money from the United States, was not for me. I was a grown-ass man, and I was going to get rich by any means possible.

As I cruised through the slum of the Gully, it saddened me to see how people were still living even after all these years. What made it worse was the fact that these politicians would come out here close to election time and would offer fake-ass promises, give out a few jobs, distribute a few bags of flour and sugar, and hand out a few dollars, just enough to grab the attention of the poor people. In return, the people would go out and vote for these dishonest politicians, thinking that a better life was going to come for them if they voted. The truth was, after the election was over, the politicians disappeared, along with all the promises that were made to the people. See, this was the reason why the community was so fucked up. There was no money coming in, and all the youths could do was turn to a life of crime, killing, raping, and robbing their own people in order to survive.

On my way, I drove past a few niggas. They were young, so more than likely, they didn't know me. I cruised to the address of my partner. I spotted him and others sitting outside a cook spot that he had. It was really a front for all the other shit he had going on.

I pulled up, then tucked my gun in my waist before I exited the car. See, the Gully was not a nice place and was definitely no place to be without a strap. I walked up to the niggas sitting outside. I noticed they were playing dominoes and talking shit to one another.

"Yo, what's up, niggas?" I said as I approached.

"Yo, Father, bless up," Gio said.

"What's up, mi linky?" my nigga Leroy said. Shit, I was happy to see Leroy. He was one of my riders in New York. He had got less time than the rest of us 'cause they really didn't hear him discussing anything on any of the tapes. He had got ten years, while the rest of us had got fifteen or more.

"Trevor, my nigga, what's good, dawg?" I said. We exchanged daps.

"Yo, boss man, we've been waiting on you so we can figure out our next move," Gio said.

"Shit. Let's get to it, then, niggas. We got shit to do."

"Yo, let's go to the back. Yo, Camille, hold the front down," Gio said.

After he said that, I saw a sexy, dark chocolate chick walk to the front. "All right, boss. I have it under control," she said as she sashayed past me, hips swinging to the sides and ass bouncing up and down. She looked familiar, but I couldn't recall where I knew her from. Our eyes locked for a quick second before she disappeared.

Damn. Who the fuck is that? I thought.

"Yo, Father, you good? You look zoned out still." Gio tapped me on the shoulder.

"Yeah, I'm good, nigga. Yo, is that shawty yours?"

"Who? Camille? Hell nah, nigga. You don't remember her?" He laughed.

"Nah. Her face looks familiar, but it's been so long, I can't call it."

"Come on. We need to handle this business first before you start worrying 'bout pussy."

Shit, that nigga was tripping. I had been gone for years, and other than the bitch he had brought to the house a few nights ago, I ain't fucked nothing else. Yeah, I was worried about getting this paper, but I planned on smashing bitches in the process.

I entered the room in the back, where I immediately spotted cameras. I noticed that they surrounded the entire building and also were focused on the street. I loved how this nigga had the shit set up. You could see everything that went on up front just by watching the TVs.

"Yo, what's the pree, Father?" Gio said.

"Yo, my niggas, y'all already know we on some money pree. Not no little bit of money, but enough money where we can live comfortably out this bitch. Y'all know how the system out here work more than I do. So we need fi put we head together and come up with the perfect plan how to get this money. The weed business too slow right now, but if it pick up, den we can dabble in that also. My main focus is the coca. Me 'ave a few connects in Miami that's willing to fuck wit' me on it, but the ting is how to get it to them without customs intercepting it—"

"Father, I love this idea, but mi 'ave one betta than that," this younger nigga, Dee Lo, said, interrupting me.

"And yuh is?" I quizzed.

"Yo, a my nephew dis, Father. 'Im cool still, and 'im know 'im ting."

"Cool. What idea you 'ave that is betta than the one I'm talkin' about?" I asked in a cold tone.

I didn't like that the little nigga didn't have the sense to shut the fuck up and wait until I was finished with what I was saying. See, these niggas must be sleeping on me, 'cause my accent ain't as raw as theirs, or maybe 'cause they felt like I wasn't one of them since I'd been gone so long.

"No disrespect still, mi genna, but coke money is good, but di scamming money is way betta," Dee Lo replied.

The entire room got quiet as the little young head spoke. I looked at him. Whatever he was saying sounded foreign to me. Since I'd been back, I'd heard niggas talking 'bout this scamming shit here and there, but I had no idea what the fuck it was, and I didn't even care. Shit, I was a drug dealer and a killer. I didn't scam people. However, since this nigga felt the need to bring it up, I decided to see what the fuck he was talking about.

"Scamming money? Nigga, I'm tryin'a build a 'millions of dollars' empire, not some five grand and bullshit-ass change."

"Father, trust me, the youth know him ting," Gio said. "Di scamming ting is the big thing now. Why you think you see all these big houses and big foreign cars popping up? A nuh drug money. Mi 'ave a brethren that make over six million in one week. One week, Father, by just using his phone. A Mobay and St. James niggas dem a eat off of it. A just now town niggas catching on. I mean, we can push di coke and start fuckin' wid di scamming ting too. A rich, we a try get rich."

His words were spinning around in my head. *Over six million in one week.* That shit seemed a little suspicious, but I knew my nigga knew his math, and we'd been rolling so long that I trusted his judgment.

I nodded slowly. "A'ight, my niggas. Y'all have me interested in dis shit. I'm fresh to this shit, so how does it work?"

"Yo, the Africans started this shit many years ago," Dee Lo informed me. "Is like you buy a spreadsheet from a connect in America or Canada. On it are names of people and their phone numbers. It's mostly rich white people. You have somebody on di team that will make the calls, informing the person that they win thousands of dollars, maybe millions, and that they'll have to send money first to process the amount they about to get. You can tell them the processing fee is anywhere from a hundred to five thousand US dollars."

I frowned. "Yo, this sound like bloodclaat fuckery to me."

"Yo, I'm a telling you, it's the business now."

"So you tellin' mi, people in America are so fucking stupid that they willin' to send money to a fucking stranger in hope that they're going to get thousands and possibly millions?"

Dee Lo shook his head enthusiastically. "Hell yeah, my genna. That is exactly what we saying. Because of dem stupid asses, we can be rich young niggas."

By the time the meeting was over, I was feeling optimistic. I had a few thousand US dollars that I had stashed away. It was time to hit the niggas up in Miami. I was ready to get shit started. They also had me sold on the scamming shit. So before I walked out of Gio's back room, I called my sister in New York and told her that I needed four brand-new laptops shipped down to me. I also copped a few new phones, which I would use for the scamming thing. The only thing I needed now was a chick to pick up the money at Western Union. This was the hard part, because I didn't know too many bitches down here and definitely none that I could trust. . . .

After I got off the phone, I walked out to the bar area, and there was that sexy bitch Camille sitting down, pretending like she was so occupied on her phone.

"Yo, shawty, lemme get a shot of Patrón," I said to her as I took a seat at the bar.

"My name is Camille," she said with a slight attitude.

"My bad, Camille. Can I get a shot of Patrón?"

"You sure can." She got up, poured a shot of Patrón, and placed it in front of me. "That will be a thousand."

I handed her a five-thousand-dollar bill. "Keep the change," I said and winked at her.

She went back to doing what she was doing before I walked in. I took out my phone and texted my nigga in Miami, letting him know that we needed to link ASAP.

"Can I get you another drink?" Camille asked me a while later. Her sexy voice echoed in my head.

"Nah, gorgeous. But how 'bout yo' number?"

"Excuse me?" She looked at me like she was shocked.

"Yo, B, stop playing games. I wan' yo' number." I spoke with my raw Jamaican accent, which was still mixed with an American accent.

"No, I don't want to give you my number. Sorry, baby," she said and then walked off.

I wasn't tripping. I knew her ass was just being careful. I took the last sip of my drink and got up from the bar. Walked out to join my niggas.

"Yo, my niggas, I'm out. I hit my nigga up, so soon as he link, things will start rolling. Also gonna check out some laptops," I announced.

We exchanged daps. Then I jumped into my car and left out. As much as I liked being around the niggas, I didn't feel too safe in the Gully. Niggas were just too grimy there, and I had learned the last time around that I couldn't trust nobody. . . .

Chapter Three

Camille

I'm so tired of living in this slum, I thought as I walked home from work. Even though it was evening time, Kingston, Jamaica, was still burning up from the hot sun.

I had been busting my ass lately, working long hours at the bar and going to various parties on the weekend and doing dance competitions. I competed against other area dancers. Lately, I'd been killing the game and winning most of the competitions, which had earned me the privilege of saving over fifty grand. However, that was a far cry from what I needed to get a nice place somewhere uptown. While the Gully would always be my home, things were starting to get out of hand. With area dons beefing with other areas, people barely wanted to be out and about after dark in the Gully. Many nights when I left the bar and walked down to my lane on Robert Avenue, I prayed to God.

Shit didn't seem like it would get any better anytime soon, 'cause it seemed like even the police were scared of coming down here. I often heard the police commissioner talking 'bout how he goin' to clean up the area, but that was just a bag of shit. Crimes had been going on down here even before I was born. Plus, the way the police were lately, they were more criminal than the dudes.

I held tight to my little purse as I walked down the street now. I had a little knife in it that couldn't do much damage, but I planned to stick it as far as I could if one of these boys ever tried to attack me. I was dead-ass tired; feet was hurting and everything. I was not goin' to complain, though, 'cause Gio had given me the job, even though a lot of other bitches had been lined up to get it. I knew Gio from when we were growing up. He moved to America but came back a few years ago, when they dipped him.

I was almost at my gate when I heard a vehicle coming up behind me. I heard the car horn honk, but I kept walking. In Jamaica, most times it was best to just hold your head straight and just mind your own business. The car pulled right in front of me and stopped.

"Yo, what the bumboclaat you doing?" I yelled, not giving a fuck who the driver was or what the repercussions were going to be for me cussing at him.

The driver's door opened, and I quickly dug into my purse and grabbed my ratchet knife. I was ready to fight for my life or die fighting.

The tall, dark, dreadlocked dude that was in the bar earlier stepped out of the car and asked, "Yo, you good?"

"Yo, what is wrong wit' yo? Why you cut me off like that?"

He was smiling like this shit was a joke, but my ass was angry as fuck. My heart was racing because I hadn't been sure if I was about to be raped, robbed, or shot.

"Yo, chill out, shawty. Get in. I'll take you home."

"You pull in front of me, and now you thinking I'm foolish enough to get into a car with a stranger? This gyal is no fool. I'll walk home. Matter of fact, my house is two houses down, so I don't need a ride."

"Yo, Camille. That's yo' name, right? Why you playing hard to get? Yo, I see you and I like you, so what's the problem?"

I stood there looking at him. I knew who he was. I remembered us growing up together. He was, like, three or four years older than me, but I remembered him. I didn't when I first saw him, but while he was back in the office area, I asked Jimmy, the bar boy, and he gladly let me know that this was the nigga that was making big moves in America and who had got torn off by the Feds. After his time in America, they had deported him to Jamaica. So yes, he looked good and all, but he had just got deported, so I knew his ass ain't got shit, and I barely got anything, so what the fuck would I want with him?

"Listen, Donavan, or Gaza, as they call you. I'm not looking for no man, and you is wasting my time. Mi tired and need to go home, so no disrespect. You look good and everything, but I'm not interested." I started walking off on him. This nigga was obviously wasting my time, and I was hungry and about to be angry.

"All right, shawty. Remember, though, I'm not giving up. I'ma make you my woman." Without saying another word, he jumped in his car and pulled off.

Who the fuck this nigga think he is, telling me he is not going to stop until he gets me? I thought. *Shit. He really got me fucked up if he thinks I'm one of these licky-licky Jamaican bitches that is frightened for a Yankee bwoy. Shit, he better ask his niggas. Camille is the real deal. . . .*

When I reached my house, I noticed my best friend and partner in crime, Sophia, was sitting on my verandah, waiting. *Oh shit*. I had forgotten I told her to meet me at my place.

"Yo, my girl, you too wicked. Why you tell me say, you walking down the lane. You 'ave me sitting out here with all these mosquitos tearing my ass up."

"My girl, I'm so sorry. I was almost at the gate when a bwoy pull him car in front a mi. Trust mi, you don't know how mi vex."

"A which bwoy that, and what he wanted?"

"Gyal, is a bwoy from foreign name Gaza. Him grow up round here, but he went to America since he's young. He just get dip, and now he's back in the place with Gio and him crew. "

"Really? How I don't know 'im?"

"He left long time before you move round here."

"So what he want with you?"

"The bwoy is looking me," I muttered through my teeth.

"So nothing is wrong wit' that. It's not like you 'ave a man. Shit, it's been a while since you get any dick."

I whipped my neck around and looked at this bitch. How the fuck she just going to say that shit?

"Gyal, you really serious right now?" I said.

"Like a heart attack. Bitch, it's time you start fucking again. Omar gone fi 'bout a year now. He's not coming back, boo boo."

I hated that she would bring up my ex, Omar. He was the one that had taken my virginity, and we'd gone steady for 'bout six years. I had thought everything was going good between us. That was until I saw posted on his WhatsApp a picture of him and a girl and someone congratulating him on his marriage. I'd never forget that Saturday. It was like my world had stopped at that moment. I remembered running from my house to Sophia's house. When she'd come to the gate, I couldn't even speak. I had just stood there and had started crying and had shown her the picture. Being that she was my bestie, she'd led me inside her house and had me lie down. I'd stayed in that position until the next day. Just the memory of that shit hurt my soul. Up to this day I hadn't laid my eyes on Omar to ask him how he could do me like that. . . .

"Hello, bitch. Back to earth," Sophia said.

"Yo, sorry. Was caught up thinking 'bout Omar and the shit he pulled."

"Bitch, let Omar go suck his stinking pussy mother. I hate that bwoy with a passion."

Sophia was not joking when she said that. After the shit went down, she'd gone to war with him on WhatsApp, IG, and Facebook. I think Omar had ended up blocking her, and since he had never made it back to the area, he didn't have much to worry about.

"I hear you, my girl, but after all di shit I went through wit' Omar, I'm not sure I'm ready to date another man so soon."

"Bitch, you know who you are? You is Camille, the rassclaat best dancer in town and country. When gyal see you, they salute you. You better boss up and take what's rightfully yours. Stop worry 'bout a dirty, no-good-ass bwoy. Omar fi dead long time."

I looked at her and smiled. I swore I didn't know what I would do without her. Some people in the community said she was messy and stayed in drama, but I saw it differently. Sophia was originally from Tivoli Gardens, and she was just real. She didn't bite her tongue and would tell you exactly what was on her mind. Trust, this bitch was not scared.

"Anyway, I'm dying of hunger. Do you want to walk out on the scheme and let us see if di chicken man is out there?" Sophia said.

"Yeah, let me change my clothes real quick."

"All right, Muma. Hurry up. Dem mosquito are deadly bad."

I opened the door to my little one-bedroom apartment and rushed inside. I grabbed a pair of little shorts and a small tank top and quickly got dressed. Within minutes, me and my bestie was walking up the road, gossiping about everything that went on in the Gully.

After we got the chicken, we walked back to my house, where we sat down on the verandah and ate. The entire time we were eating, my mind was thinking about what Sophia had said. I mean, I'd been trying not to date anyone, because I was still hoping and praying that Omar would come back to me. But my friend was right. That nigga had dissed me and now belonged to another bitch. What the fuck was I waiting for? It might be too late, though, 'cause I did blow Gaza off twice. A nigga like him could get any bitch he wanted, so what the fuck this nigga wanted with little old me . . . ?

When we were done eating, Sophia stood up. "Yo, bitch, it's getting late, so I'm going to my yard. You know how Oneil get brindle when he come in before me, and true, I'm not in the mood to fight him tonight. Plus, tomorrow night your show, and I need mi money from him to do my hair and my nails tomorrow."

"A'ight, goody. Text me when you reach inside the house. I'm going to have a bath right now."

"All right, boo."

I watched as she walked down the street. When she was no longer in sight, I unlocked the grill and walked into my apartment. I was tired as hell, and I needed to shower and rest up because tomorrow night was a big night for me. I had a dance contest, and I would receive fifty grand if I won. I knew that one of the girls I was competing against was a big-time dancer who used to roll with the Spice dance crew, so the pressure was on. I knew I had to practice my moves and also come up with some new moves that nobody had ever seen before. I looked in the mirror. Was I ready for this?

Hell yeah, bitch, you ready, a voice echoed in my head.

My freshly done weave was in a bun, and my body was looking good dressed in a bodycon. I planned to perform tonight in a white jumpsuit from Victoria's Secret. This was my night, and I was shining like the diamond I knew I was. Some of these bitches in the dance contest did this shit to pass the time, but this was my way of getting out of the ghetto. The more battles I won, the more my name would circulate. I was hoping that one day one of these entertainers would come looking for me to be in their videos or go on tour with them. Yeah, I was only a girl from the ghetto, but that didn't stop me from dreaming big.

I watched as bitches pointed fingers and whispered among themselves in the club's lobby. I didn't even acknowledge them. Instead, I swung the little ass and hips that God had blessed me with and made my way to the dressing room. Then I dialed Sophia.

"Bitch, where you at?" I asked when she answered the phone.

"Yo, I'm two minutes from the club. Are you there?"

"Yes. I'm in the changing room. Hurry up and come on."

I hung the phone up and changed my clothes. I was almost finished dressing when this one bitch that I had beaten numerous times walked in. I could smell trouble from a mile away. This bitch, Anika, had been salty the last time I beat her, and she had kept yelling at the judges that they were cheating for me. The bitch had gone as far as threatening me. I hurried and put my legs into the pants part of the jumpsuit and pulled it up. I pretended like I was stunning the bitch, but all along I was reaching for my razor in my wallet. I placed it under my tongue. This was a trick that I had learned early on. See, when you grew up in the ghetto, you had to learn how to defend yourself.

"Yo, Marie, see the dutty gyal here that steal my spot last time?" Anika yelled to a bitch that had walked into the dressing room behind her.

"Eh, is that her? Look on the old parasite. They stole yo' spot, goody. After this gyal don't even look like she can dance," her big, bad friend commented.

"Yo, bitch, I win that fair and square," I told Marie. "I beat your friend three time, and tonight I'm going to beat her for the fourth time. I'm a good dancer. I don't have to steal anything."

Marie glared at me. "Is it me this underprivileged gyal talking to?"

This bitch Anika stepped to my face. I didn't think twice. I pulled the razor out of my mouth and just went in.

"Oh my God! This gyal cut you, goody!" was all I heard.

I opened my eyes and saw that I had blood all over my dance clothes. I looked over, and I saw the bitch holding her face. She was screaming.

I grabbed my bag and stuffed my things in there.

"She a try to leave. Hold the gyal and beat her," someone said, pointing at me.

"Nobody better not put a bloodclaat hand on her. Yo, come on." Sophia grabbed my hand and pulled me through the crowd that had gathered in the dressing room.

We raced to the lobby and then out the front door of the club. The people in front of the building were not aware of what was going on, because they had been standing around, talking and drinking. The second we were outside, Sophia started flagging down a taxi. The taxis that went by zoomed past us, so more than likely they were filled with customers. I happened to look back and saw security running into the building. I knew that by now everybody was aware of what had gone down in there.

"Come on! We have to get away from here," I told Sophia.

We decided to run across the street in front of the club, but that meant we would have to dodge all these speeding cars. We waited for a gap in the flow of traffic and then ran as fast as we could. We had made it to the other side of the street when I noticed the BMW. It was the car that Gaza drove. I walked over to the car and looked inside. He was sitting in there. I guessed he had just pulled up. I didn't know he frequented this scene.

He climbed out of the car when he saw me. "Whaddup, shawty? I see we meet again." He smiled at me.

"Listen, I need a ride out of here," I told him.

"What's good?" He looked at me suspiciously.

"I got into it with a gyal in the club, and I end up cutting her. Now they're after me."

"Oh, word. Get it in, yo." He looked around.

I was about to get in the car when Sophia grabbed my arm. "Who is this? You know him?" She was looking at me suspiciously now.

"This is the same youth that I was telling you about. The other man. Come on," I said.

We all got in the car, and he pulled off. He drove past the club, and the crowd was gathered around the entrance, but we couldn't see anything else. This was some bullshit.

"Yo, what happen in there with you and the bitches?" he asked once the club was in his rearview mirror.

"Yo, I come up here to compete in the dance contest. This gyal that I beat three times have it in for me. She jump up in my face, along with her friend. I tried to ignore them, but the bitch start disrespecting. So I pull the razor out my mout' and slice di gyal in her face. A long time, I give that gyal. Whole lot of passes."

"Yo, goody, I'm sorry I was late. 'Cause, trust mi, if I was there, that gyal couldn't come up inna yuh face like dat. Trust me," Sophia said. I could tell by her tone that she was pissed off.

"I didn't know you is a bad gyal, mon." He burst out laughing.

"Why you laughing like it's a joke thing? What if they call the police? I'll be locked up," I said in an annoyed tone.

"Yo, relax . . . A Jamaica this, so them bitches ain't callin' no police. If anything, you just have to be prepared to fuck them up again."

"I'm not afraid of these bitches. I'm angry because tonight I'm s'pposed to get fifty grand if I won. This is how I make my money. I'm an independent gyal, and this gyal come fuck with me and fuck up my thing. Yo, I'm vex bad."

"Yo, chill out, babes. Fifty grand? That's nothing, babes. Just easy," he said.

He was saying that shit 'cause he probably got money, but I didn't have money like that. I made a few dollars at the bar, but dancing was my thing to get me up out of the ghetto.

"Y'all ladies going home?"

"Yeah, if you don't mind. Drop me home please. I 'ave this gyal blood all ova my clothes," I said.

The rest of the ride was quiet; I was too fucking upset to keep on talking. With the anger that

I was feeling right now, I could definitely kill that bitch. Why the fuck would she decide to mess with me? I was not a troublemaker. I made my little money and took care of myself. Tears wanted to flow, but my pride wouldn't let me cry in front of a nigga that I barely knew. So I used everything in me to hold it in.

Twenty minutes later he pulled up at the house. But wait, how the fuck did he know exactly where I lived at? *Hmm. Let me find out this nigga been doing his homework*, I thought.

"Here you go, ladies."

"Tanks," Sophia said and jumped out.

"Thank you. I appreciate it," I told him. I was about to exit the car when he grabbed my arm.

"Yo, B. Take my number and link mi."

"Come on, Gaza. Mi appreciate what you just do for me, but I just tell you I don't want no man."

"Camille, fuck that nigga that hurt you. I'm a man, not him. Yo, take this number and link mi," he said in a serious tone.

Chapter Four

Gaza

Ever since I had laid eyes on the catty at the bar a week ago, I couldn't seem to get her off my mind. The first thing that had caught my eye was her phat ass. I had blinked twice to make sure I wasn't tripping. She was a little cutie, too. As I took a sip of my liquor, I'd scoped her out from head to toe. To be honest, there were a lot of bad bitches in Jamaica, but she was sexy, with a hot look.

I ain't goin' to lie. I'd been kind of irritated when she turned me down. Either she had a man or she was playing hard to get. Being the nigga I was, though, I wasn't goin' to sit around and beg no bitch to be with me. Shit, everywhere I went lately on the island, bitches were hollering at me. I had shot her a look and had walked out of the bar. In due time she would come to her senses. I hoped she didn't wait too long.

I was so busy ripping and running and trying to get this money rolling in, I barely had time to sleep. Money was on my mind hard. Shit, a nigga could sleep when I hit a couple of million, US, of course. Shit. I ain't seen my dawg Gio in a few days, so I decided to get dressed and go link him. I pulled on a shirt and shorts and gave him a call.

"Yo, mi genna, you at the spot?" I asked when he picked up.

"No, mi daddy. Mid eh dung by Waltham Park Road. Mi a eat a fish enuh."

"Oh word. Yo, mi hungry too enuh. A'ight, mi a cum link yuh."

"A'ight, mi daddy," he said before we hung up.

I got in my car and head toward Waltham Park. I could hear my belly growling from being hungry. I loved how everything was working out, and I just needed to rap with my nigga, since he was my partner and right-hand man. I was still new in the place, but he had been here and was more familiar with a lot of shit that went on. He even had a few police on his payroll. That was definitely a plus, because we needed to know ahead of time when shit was about to hit the fan.

I spotted Gio's car when I pulled up at the little fish spot. I parked beside him and got out. I walked in the restaurant and immediately caught sight of him.

"Whaddup, son?" I greeted him when I reached his table.

"I'm here, Father," he said, stretching his hand out. We exchanged daps.

I took a seat beside him. He waved to the cook to come over to us.

"Yo, give mi brethren the biggest fish that you have," he told the cook when she reached our table.

"Let me get a Guinness too," I added.

After the cook handed me a cold Guinness, Gio and I sat there, just rapping about shit in general. We were in a restaurant, so we were careful not to discuss no personal shit. I had taken a glance around when I first sat down, and had seen that motherfuckers were sitting around, just being nosy and shit.

My fish was done in no time, and I wasted no time in digging in after the cook placed it in front of me. I really didn't realize how famished I was until now.

"Damn. You is starving, mon. You need a woman over at the yard to cook for you," Gio observed.

"You see it too?"

We burst out laughing. Shit. I ain't never been shy about no food, and I wasn't going to start now.

After we finished eating, we sat there drinking a few more Guinness. Then we left out.

"Yo, get in real quick," I told Gio as I motioned to my car.

We both had the same plan to take over the Gully and surrounding areas. There was a lot of money to be made if we just stayed on top of our shit. We had decided to put our minds together and get shit accomplished.

Once we were both seated in my car, I turned to my right-hand man. "Yo, Gio, fuck these niggas out here. We ain't new to this shit. Matter of fact, we been doing this shit for a minute now. We goin' to show these niggas how it supposed to be done."

"Yo, Father, I love how you thinking. It sound good, but we might have to strong-arm the spots and be ready fo' war," Gio said.

"B, I'm ready fo' whatever. These niggas have no idea, we natural-born killers."

"True. This is a new ball game. Since the scamming thing start, it's like bloodshed everywhere. These niggas are on some other shit. We can't trust none of them, Father."

"Yo, you is my brother. You is the only nigga I trust." I gave that nigga a serious look so he would know how dead ass I really was.

"From day one, you already know, a family we say."

I knew taking over these areas wasn't going to be an easy task, but we had the manpower and the guns, and in due time we'd have the paper to secure all those spots.

"Yo, I need a favor from you," I said.

"Anything."

"Yo, the catty that work in your bar . . ."

"Who you talking 'bout? Camille? I know you checking for her."

"Yeah, mon. The other night some shit pop off at the spot she was at, and she beg me for a ride home."

He looked over at me. "Nigga, those type of gyal are top notch. You have to come correct."

"I don't have no problem with that. I want her bad."

He just laughed at me. This nigga must not have noticed that I was dead-ass serious.

"Yo, son, I need to find out what clown she fucks wit'. Not that it matter, 'cause I'ma take her from that nigga."

"She don't 'ave no man. She used to mess around wit' a nigga, and the nigga ran off with another gyal. She took it real hard still."

"I got her. I'm not going to run off. I just need you to put in a good word for me," I said.

"I got you. A'ight, I have some moves to make. We can link up later."

"A'ight, yo."

He got out of the car, and I pulled off. That nigga thought I was fooling around, only 'cause he knew my reputation back in New York.

Time waited on no one, so I returned my focus to what I knew best. I couldn't let pussy get in the way of what I was trying to accomplish. Even though I was feeling the catty, I wasn't desperate. Lately, I had had different bitches spending the night with me. Also, I knew once I started stacking this bread, bitches were goin' to be there.

Shit started rolling. I was shipping keys of coke off to Miami and New York almost every week. My people out there was loving it. The thing was, it was a risky business, and costly, just to get it on the boat without getting on the radar of the Coast Guard. I knew sending shit to the United States was also dangerous. The Feds could be the ones to intercept the cargo, and shit could get sticky. I swear, I had to be extra careful, 'cause going back to prison was not an option I was trying to explore.

The demand for the raw coke had us working overtime. There were days when I barely slept or made it in the house. I was also fucking with the ganja. I had found a ganja farmer out in St. Elizabeth, and I had started getting ten pounds. I really didn't do a lot of business as far as selling shit to the locals. The police was hot out here; plus, the weed market out here was oversaturated.

I walked in the office we had set up in the back of the bar. The two dudes and the chick was working the phones. So far, we had collected over eight grand US from people who thought they were sending money in order to receive their winnings. I was new to this, but I fully understood how it worked now. This was way easier than I had thought. If they continued like this, that business would soon be booming too.

I sat down and started going through the books, checking the numbers. I did not realize that shit was about to get sticky.

Pop! Pop! Pop!

I heard gunshots ringing out. I grabbed my burner from my waist and ran out of the office. When I got to the front of the bar, I saw a nigga lying on the floor. I ran past him and outside. All I could see was a CBR bike speeding away from the scene.

Fuck! I rushed back in to see who the fuck that was that was lying there on the floor. By then the people that were in the bar had surrounded him.

"Somebody call a taxi! Please this man a-go dead right now," I shouted.

The scene was horrible. I realized the victim was a guy named Ratty, one of the little soldiers that was on our team. *Shit*. I knew I had to act fast. . . . In no time the police would be storming in here. I needed to get him up out of here fast.

"Aye, you got a ride?" I said to a nigga that was standing around. "Here. Two hundred US dollars. Run him down by the hospital."

"He's not going to make it, Father."

"Yo, I never ask you no fucking question," I snarled. "Take the man out of the place before the bloodclaat pigs them come through. We don't need this kind of heat up in here right now."

Without saying another word, a few niggas grabbed Ratty and carried him outside.

I looked around at everybody that was standing around. "Yo, I'ma need y'all to keep y'all mouth shut," I shouted, with venom in my voice.

I then rushed to the back. "Yo, we need to shut everything down right now. Ratty just got shot, and we need to move out before Babylon come through. Grab di computer them and put in my car. Operation shut down till further notice."

"A'ight, boss man," said one of the dudes who had been working the phones.

I then dialed Gio's number, but he wasn't picking up. I didn't have time to hang out around here when shit was about to get real. I cleared everybody out of the building and locked the grill. I then jumped in my car and pulled off. On my way out, I saw a few police cars pulling into the lane. I held my head straight and kept driving. I had my burner on me; plus, I had all these computers with numbers on them. This shit alone carried a lot of jail time.

My phone started ringing.

"Yo, Father," Gio said as soon as I picked up the phone.

"Yo, I'm on the way to the crib."

"Cool. I'ma link wit' you in a few."

I could tell by the tone of his voice that he was aware of what had just gone on. I already knew how he got down, and I knew shit was about to get real sticky. I made it to the house, put the code in at the gate, and pulled in. After I came to a stop and turned off the car, I jumped out, grabbed the computers, brought them into the house, and stashed them in one of the spare bedrooms.

I walked into the kitchen and poured me a glass of Hennessy. I then rolled a blunt while I waited on Gio to pull up. My mind was all over the place. It had been years that I'd seen a nigga shot. But I just knew that we were goin' to have to go to war over this shit. There was no way we could let that shit slide like that.

Gio's car pulled up to the gate. I unlocked the grill, went outside, and opened the gate for him. He parked, and then we both walked in the house.

"What's good, Daddy?" he said. We exchanged daps.

"Yo, you hear what happen to Ratty?"

"Yeah. 'Im sister just call mi phone. Ratty didn't make it," he said, choking up.

"Dawg, you serious?" I lowered my head. "Yo, di shit happen so fast. I come through and passed Ratty out front. I went to the back to check on the workers them and to see how things were going on. A few minutes later, I hear gunshot, so I reach for my burner and run out front. By the time I got outside, I see the pussy them car speeding down the lane, but too much people was on the lane, so I couldn't even bust at them. By time I go back inside the place, I realize say a Ratty them shot up. That's when I pay a youth to transport him to the hospital. I hurry up and lock up di place before the pussy them show up."

"Jah know, star, Ratty is family. Why 'im even a live this lifestyle, you know? Yo them pussyhole niggas going to pay with their lives. From them mother to them rass pickney, they're going to pay," he yelled in a cold but fierce tone.

"Yo, you already know say, if a blood you say, then that's what it is."

"Yo, Father. I feel like it's the bwoy them from First Avenue. It's been a minute since them niggas been trying to get at us."

"Yo, my nigga, soon as we find out which pussy do it, we gonna handle that. If they violate one, then they violate all of us." I paused for a moment. "Yo, hit da blunt here, and calm down. The place is hot right now, so we need to lay low for a few days. We 'ave too much to lose right now."

"Yeah."

I knew he was hearing me, but I had no idea if he was taking me seriously. Gio had always been a hothead. I was the one that remained calm in the midst of war. It wasn't always this easy for me, but over the years I had learned that in order to get shit done, you had to plan and then execute when the time was right. Yeah, we could go to the Gully and shoot up everything and everybody, but what good would that do if the niggas were not around? All we would do was bring heat to us, something we couldn't afford. I got a one-thousand-US-dollar business running right now, and running around without a plan intact would only fuck up our money and have the police all over our shit. We had to move differently.

We kicked it for about an hour before Gio left out. I knew he was angry, and before he left, I tried my best to talk some sense into his head. I could tell he had murder on his mind. The thing was, he was my brother, and if he was going to war, best believe my ass got to go to war also. The thought of that bothered my mind. Here I was, trying to get rich, and now beef was about to kick off.

After he left, my phone started ringing non-stop. I was tired of picking it up, but I did, anyway. People were just hearing about what had happened earlier, and most of them wanted to know what the fuck we were going to do about it. After the first ten calls, I was pissed off that they were hitting me up, so I kept pressing IGNORE, but the phone continued to ring.

"Yo!" I yelled into the phone after vowing that this would be the last call I took.

"Sorry. I must reach you at a bad time." The sweet, sexy voice of Camille rang through my ear.

"No, beautiful. I didn't realize it was you. How you doing?"

"I'm good. I heard what happen to Ratty today, so I call to check on you."

"Yo, I'm good, babes. The pussy them violate still. But you know, we good. So when am I going to see you?"

"When you wan' to see me?"

"How 'bout right now?"

"Right now, you know I'm in the Gully. Are you coming to pick me up?"

"Nah, but if you grab a taxi, I'll pay the fare," I said.

"All right then. Text mi your address. I'm going to bathe, and then I'll be on the way."

"A'ight, bet," I said before hanging up.

Yes! I knew it was only a matter of time before she came around. I knew she knew I wasn't going to chase her ass around anymore. I took a quick shower before she came over. Kingston was burning up, and even though the AC was running, it was still humid. Sometimes I missed the wintertime in America. Speaking of America, I had been thinking about it lately. This was where I had spent most of my life. I had a brethren that was telling me about a link he had that could get me back in the United States through the Mexico border. The shit cost a lot of money. I wasn't ready to check that out yet. I got shit that I needed to handle out here. Plus, life was good right now.

About two hours later, a taxi pulled up at the gate. I walked outside, stepped through the gate. "How much is it?"

"It's two grand, boss," said the driver.

I counted off the two grand, handed it to him. Camille stepped out of the cab and walked around to greet me.

"What's up, beautiful?"

"I'm here. Wow. This yo' house? It's nice," she said as she walked to the gate to get a better look at my baby mansion.

"Yeah, this where I lay my head."

We walked back in the house, and I locked the grill. My eyes strayed, and I looked her over from head to toe. She had on little booty shorts, which revealed her ass cheeks. Shit, I was thinking of all the positions that I could have her in before the day was over.

"Yo, this is nice, Gaza. You live by yourself?" she said as she followed me to the living room.

"Why? You wan' to come live with me?" I asked jokingly as we both took a seat.

"No, I 'ave my own yard. It's not big and fancy like this, but I'm comfortable."

"I hear you. You want something to drink?"

"Yeah. What you 'ave?"

"Everything. Liquor, soda, water, milk. Your choice," I told her.

"Let me get a soda please."

I got up and walked into the kitchen and grabbed her a can of Coca-Cola. I grabbed me a Heineken. We went out on the verandah and sat and talked, and she shared a lot of memories of Ratty with me.

"Yo, I'm hungry. You couldn't bring me some lunch?" I joked after we had talked for about an hour.

"You know, when you call me, I just finish washing some clothes. I'm not fortunate like you to have a washing machine, so I had to stand in the hot sun and scrub these clothes with my hands."

"Well, you could have called, and I would've let you use my machine," I told her.

"I'll definitely keep that in mind. So what you feel like eating?"

"Yo, I'm tired of box food. Shit don't even taste the same anymore. It's like the people them not seasoning the food good anymore."

"Yeah, is not that. Is just that everybody want to be a cook now. It's more of a hustle for people to make a money. What do you have in the kitchen can cook?"

I shrugged. "I don't even know. The helper usually cook for me, but I gave her the day off to go visit her family in Portland. But you can look what's in there. Come on."

We both got up, and I took her hand and led her into the kitchen. I opened the freezer.

"I see chicken, steak, and fish in the freezer," I said. "I know I got flour and rice in the cupboard."

"Hmm, I can make some steam fish and dumpling. You have any green banana?"

"Yeah, I think I see a half a hand. Look by the side of the cupboard."

She shook her head. "Yes, only a few, but that's all we need."

"Seasoning and everything is in the cupboard or the fridge," I noted. "Get familiar with the kitchen."

"Uh-huh. You lucky I'm hungry."

"I love a woman that knows her way around the kitchen."

"Whatever, bwoy. Lots of bitches don't know how to cook, and they still get a man."

"Well, I'm not one of those niggas. Any bitch I fucks with got to know her way around the kitchen. Me is a man that love my cook food. It don't have to be every day, but most days."

"Go on 'bout your business while I cook this food."

I smiled at her and walked out of the kitchen and back onto the verandah. Just being around her definitely gave me a good vibe.

***

"This food smell delicious," I said as I sat down at the dining room table.

"Take a bite. It taste delicious too." She giggled.

She didn't have to say it twice, 'cause a nigga was famished. I dug into the food that was in front of me. She was right. This shit was delicious. I had to give it to her, she was a beast in the kitchen. We talked, laughed, and ate. I had to say this was the first time in a long time that I had felt so relaxed around a female. It seemed as if I'd known her my entire life.

After dinner, she cleaned up the kitchen, and then we sat on the verandah, drinking and smoking.

"Here. Take a drag off this ganja." I offered her the blunt.

"Bwoy, I don't smoke. Nah, let me correct that. I tried smoking about a year ago, and I almost die from the smoke. My ass never tried it again."

"C'mon, I'll teach you. Take it." I shoved the blunt in her hand.

I watched as she cautiously took a pull from the blunt.

"Take short pulls and exhale slowly," I instructed.

That didn't go too well, because she started to cough.

"You a'ight. I told you to take your time," I said.

"I did," she managed to say in between coughing and almost choking.

I got up and walked into the kitchen, where I poured her some water. I brought it back out to her. "Here, drink this. I see you still an amateur," I joked.

"Boy, fuck you. I almost died." She took the glass and took sips of the water.

After her coughing calmed down, we burst out laughing.

"You tried to kill me on the first date," she joked.

"Shit, I told yo' greedy ass to take it slow. You the one that decide you want to smoke like you a pro." My phone started ringing just then, so I grabbed it. "Yo."

"What's the pree, Father?" Gio said.

"I'm at the crib, chilling."

"You not touching the road? A few of us going to a round-robin on Maxfield Avenue. Was checking to see if you want to forward."

"Nah, I'm kind of busy tonight. I'll link up with you niggas tomorrow."

"Word, a female must be over at the crib." He burst out laughing.

"Go ahead, nigga. I'ma hit you in the a.m."

"Bless up, Father."

"One."

While I was on the phone, Camille had wandered into the living room. I headed there and turned my focus back to sexy-ass, hot-body Camille, who was now sitting on my couch, revealing her sexy legs, which were wide open, exposing her fat pussy. I could tell she was tipsy from drinking two bottles of rum cream.

"Miss Camille, so let me cut to the chase. A nigga is checking for you. I don't want a fuck partner. I get pussy when I want it. I want a woman to be loyal to me and to be by my side."

"Hmmm, Gaza, you a fine-ass nigga, seem to have money, just come from America. What I can't seem to understand is, Why me? Why a poor little ghetto girl like me? I mean, I know you must have plenty of bitches chasing you and shit. You know how thirsty these Jamaican bitches are."

"Camille, fuck the rest of these bitches. Like I said, it ain't about the pussy. I see the qualities that I'm looking for in a woman. I understand that you been through some shit, but I'm not that nigga. I'm not goin' to hurt you." I took a seat on the other end of the couch.

"So I see someone been telling you my business, huh?"

"Well, niggas know I like you. Plus, that shit is public knowledge. I don't give a fuck 'bout yo' past, though. All I'm trying to do is to be the one that makes you smile. We can build a life together. We can do great together. You know the struggle, and I know the struggle. Together we can make millions, and, shit, we can go to any country we want."

She stared me in the eyes. "Gaza, can I ask you a question?"

"Yeah."

"Why they dip you?"

"So I see someone was telling you my business. Well, to be honest, I was locked up for thirteen years. I was one of the biggest drug dealers in New York. Shit got hot, and a nigga snitched on Gio and the rest of the crew."

"Oh, okay . . ."

"Yo, Camille, my lifestyle ain't got nothing to do with my feelings for you. I ain't gonna be in these streets forever. My plan is to make a couple million and get out of it."

"I hear you, but I don't, Gaza. This a dangerous lifestyle you living. Things change from when you last live out here. Guns are everywhere, and the drug game and scamming money really have these niggas killing one another. Every day on the news, it's a lot of killing. It's disgusting. We can't even walk on the road at night anymore."

I nodded. "I hear you, babes, but you grow up in the ghetto, so you know the struggle. We have to grind and get it whichever way we can. We can't just sit around and depend on others to give us a food. We have to go out here and get it."

"Yeah, you right. It's just that I couldn't bear to hear that anything bad happen to you. I see girls losing their man every day. Just like Ratty baby mother. Is three youths she left with to take care of by herself. Shit is not fair."

"Baby girl, listen, every soldier in the streets knows the consequences, and even though it's a fucked-up situation, it's part of the life. I can't sit here and tell you that ain't shit going to pop off. If I did, I would be lying, but I'm just asking you for a chance."

I reached over and started rubbing her legs. She didn't resist, which let me know it was okay to proceed. I moved closer to her and started kissing her passionately. She held my head and started kissing me back. I pulled her onto my lap and then explored her body with my hands. I started massaging her breasts while inhaling the exotic scent of her body. Then I kissed her neck while I started unbuttoning the blouse she was wearing.

She suddenly stood up, grabbed my hands, and pulled me toward her. She locked her lips onto mine and started kissing me. I didn't waste any time. I picked her up and carried her to the bedroom. I gently laid her on the bed, then slowly undressed her, removing all her clothes, leaving her small-cup breasts out in the open. I took a few seconds to admire her sexy physique. Then I lowered myself next to her and massaged her breasts. She lay there peacefully as I took one and placed it in my mouth. Her eyes were speaking volumes to me: it was like she was screaming at me, but in a great way. I wasn't in no rush. I took my time, using my tongue to dance slowly around her nipple. She let out a few soft moans, and I used my teeth and nibbled a bit on her breast. I then reached down with my other hand and slid two fingers into her pussy, which was soaking wet. I worked her wet pussy with my fingers. I was working magic with my body without actually sexing her.

"Ooh-wee," she moaned as she ground on my fingers. "Damn, Gaza. I want you bad," she whispered in my ear.

"So what you waiting on, babes?" I whispered back to her.

That was what I needed to hear from her. I started kissing her stomach, then made my way down to her navel and beyond. I took a few seconds to inhale the natural scent of her pussy before I entered it with my mouth. I used my tongue to lick her clit. I started kissing her pussy passionately, making love to it slowly. Her body started shivering as she moaned.

"Please, Gaza, baby, fuck me please. Please give me the dick," she pleaded.

I loved how my name rolled off her tongue, but I wasn't ready to stop sucking on her pussy. Instead, the louder her moans got, the harder I sucked on her clit. Her pussy was fat and juicy, and this made it easier for me to suck on it the way I wanted to. Her legs started shivering more as juice flowed out of her body and onto my face. I didn't move an inch. Instead, I used my tongue to clean every drop of her sweet cum off her pussy.

I then lay next to her on the bed and pulled her over to me. "C'mon, babes. Come ride this dick for me."

She wasted no time; she got on top of me and slid down on my pole. She starting moving her hips in a circular fashion, which made my dick reach every corner inside of her. I held on to her hips, keeping them in place, while I thrust in and out of her. Her pussy was so wet that at one point my dick slipped out a little, and she hurriedly slid down farther on it until it was all the way up in her.

"Aweee," she moaned as she bounced up and down on the dick.

"Damn, baby. This pussy is good," I whispered to her as I dug deeper in her wet, tight pussy.

I flipped her over on her back; then I got on top her. After lifting her legs and putting them on my shoulders, I was in a much better position to tear her walls down, and I did just that. I wasn't here to play with the pussy or have her thinking I was one of them niggas that didn't know what to do with the pussy.

"Damn, baby. I want to be your woman. I want you," she blurted out, shocking the hell out of me.

I didn't respond. Shit, after having a taste of this pussy, I planned on making it mine. I held her legs tighter as my veins got larger, and I started thrusting harder. I knew then that I was about to bust, even though I had tried my best to go a little longer. I couldn't hold it in any longer; the pussy was too good, and the wetness only made it easier for me to cum. Within seconds, I busted all up in her. I had thought about pulling out, but the pussy was too good and was clinging to my dick.

Afterward, I rolled over on my back, tried to catch my breath.

"You good?" I quizzed as I rubbed her hair.

"Yes. You tear my pussy up. That dick too big."

"It ain't too big, babes. You just have to get used to it, that's all."

"You ain't gonna use that big dick and stretch out my little needle eye."

We both burst out laughing. Shawty was funny as hell.

"Come on. Let's go shower," I said after a few minutes.

The fucking continued in the shower. I lifted her up, and she wrapped her legs around me and rode the dick. Within minutes, I was exploding up in her again.

After we took a shower together, we decided to chill together for the rest of the evening. We drank more, and I smoked a few blunts back-to-back. We spent the evening getting to know each other in a more intimate way. It was definitely a breath of fresh air and a change from all the drama that had been going on.

Chapter Five

Camille

I heard a loud banging outside, and I jumped up out of my sleep. I grabbed my phone and looked at the time. *Shit*. It was after 11:00 a.m. How the hell did I manage to sleep this late? I was usually up bright and early every morning. I moved my curtain and peeked out the window. I was trying to see who the hell was outside banging like that.

"Gyal, I know you're in there. Come open up the grill," said my annoying-ass bestie, Sophia.

Oh shit. My head was pounding, and my eyes were hurting. I felt like someone had hit me over the head with a stick. That was when I remembered all those drinks I had had with Gaza the night before. The taxi had dropped me off at home this morning, around seven o' clock. I threw a robe on and looked around for the key to open the grill. I finally found it and trudged over to the front door.

"Gyal, I know you not in no bed, sleeping this time of day," Sophia said as soon as I opened the door and stepped outside.

"I have a damn headache, and yes, I was sleeping. You know that's why we have phones, to call someone before you pop up at their house."

"Bitch, fuck off. That shit doesn't apply to me. A bitch was worried about you. Last thing you told me is you about to take a taxi and go uptown to see that dude. When I ain't hear from you by 'bout twelve o'clock last night, I start calling ya phone. It rang a few times, then straight to voicemail. Bitch, I started to panic."

"You are so crazy, bitch. I didn't come home until this morning. And I got straight in the bed, head pounding," I said.

"So, my girl, you give up the pussy?"

"Bitch, did I give the pussy up? Listen, that Yankee bwoy suck my pussy so damn good. Bitch, when I tell you my whole body was shaking out of control, I thought I was having a damn seizure."

"Bitch, oh my God. How big was the dick?"

"That nigga dick was huge," I revealed. "Bitch, my pussy hurting right now. I like him and all, but I'm not sure I can keep fucking him. That nigga going to stretch my entire insides out."

"Bitch, fuck that. You is a hot gyal that wind up in dance. Shit, you have to learn to wind all over the dick. Don't be out here embarrassing me and shit. You need to make sure you fuck that nigga good. That way, he will come back."

"Bitch, I did, but I'm paying for that shit now . . . Bitch, you should see where that nigga live. That fucking house big as hell and nice. Upstairs and downstairs."

"Bitch, if you fuck him good, you might be moving up there with him soon. Did he ask you to suck his dick?"

"Bitch, nah, and if he did, it would've be no. Camille don't suck dick," I replied.

"Well, you better get with the program. You can't expect the nigga to suck on your pussy, and you don't return the favor. Every gyal a Jamaica a suck them man dick. Don't let a gyal suck the man away from you."

"Bitch, first off, I got good, tight, wet pussy. If I don't suck his dick, it's no biggie. Furthermore, I don't know how to suck dick."

"Bitch, watch YouTube. Everything you need to know is on there. Trust me, the first time you do it, you might feel crazy, but practice make perfect," she informed me.

"What a way you know?"

"Bitch, ain't no shame in my game. I been sucking dick and getting fuck in my ass. I don't hold back when it comes to me satisfying my man. Right now I'm thinking about giving Oneil a threesome for his birthday."

I looked at that bitch like she had lost her mind. It was one thing to be sucking dick, but to be thinking about getting with another bitch, that was a whole other level.

"What? Why you looking at me like that? Listen, Camille, I love sex, and I don't mind letting a bitch suck on my pussy. I have one life to live, and I'm going to make sure I live it the best way I can. I don't care. As long as me and my man happy with it, we good."

"I hear you, bitch. I mean, whatever floats your boat is cool with me. Anyway, what are you up to?"

"Not a thing. Going to run downtown to grab some stuff from the market. Listen, it's a lot of shit going on around here. I heard First Street niggas were the ones that kill Ratty. The police run up in a few houses yesterday. I don't have a good feeling." She sighed. "Gaza didn't say anything to you about what happen to Ratty?"

I shook my head. "Girl, no. We talked a little about Ratty, but he didn't really say anything. I already know Gio and them crew wasn't going to let it go. I know some shit going to pop around here, but the police everywhere, so I think they chilling." I paused. "Girl, that's fucked up how they did him, but I heard Ratty was involve with some scamming thing. I heard the money come in and Ratty take most of the money."

"Really? These niggas are not playing 'bout this money thing. I just feel bad for Mona still, 'cause she and Ratty been going together since high school days. And the three babies don't have no father now."

"Yes, true, I feel bad for her," I said. "I heard she pack up and left the area, 'cause they still don't know what Ratty did with the money."

"Well, that's a good thing she left, 'cause these old bitch-ass niggas ain't got no heart. I swear, they will kill that girl and those babies. How the fuck they know he didn't spend the money? I mean, Ratty was a big on splurging."

"That is true . . . I just pray to God that I get to leave this fucked-up-ass area. Sophia, I'm not going to lie, when I was uptown with Gaza, it was a whole different vibe. Uptown clean, no whole lot of drama. I stood out on his balcony and was thinking that this is the life I deserve to be living. Not in this ghetto, where people don't respect you and your life is constantly in danger. I'm ready to get some more dance competition, so I can move up out of here. I'm going to give myself six months to move."

"I been thinking the same thing too, Camille. I told Oneil to let us move. We can move to Portmore or Greater Portmore. But he keep talking about he's trying to save his money. I'ma give him an ultimatum, 'cause I'm tired of living in fear. Not sure when it's going to be my life. Before I lose my life down here, I rather go back to the Gardens. Things kind of cool down after the Dudus situation."

"Bitch, I feel you. I ain't goin' to lie, Sophia. This is where I was born and raised, but I'm tired of all this senseless killing that takes place down here. I want a brand-new life, for real."

"I feel you, boo. Well, it seems like you're going to get that real soon. Gaza seems to really like you. All I'm asking you is, don't forget about your bitch when you get all rich and are living up in the hills."

"Bitch, cut it out. I don't even know where me and Gaza relationship heading. I mean, I like him. Shit, I like him a lot. But niggas like him don't keep one woman, and I ain't about to have no matey. I'm too old to be sharing dick with the next bitch."

"Camille, baby, listen, this your chance. You fucking with a boss nigga. Even if you don't want to do it for love, do it for security. This is your meal ticket to get out of here and don't look back."

I nodded. "I hear you, boo. Anyways, this damn headache is killing me. I think I need some tea and something to eat."

"Yeah, and I need to jump on this taxi so I can get downtown before the rush. I will call you when I come back over here."

"Okay, girl."

I walked back into my house after Sophia left. Lord, I was never drinking again if this was how I was going to feel afterward. I checked my phone to see if Gaza had called or messaged me. He hadn't. I felt a little disappointed. I wondered if he was thinking about the time we spent together or if this was just a fling to him. One of my biggest fears was being rejected after I opened up my soul to him. I brushed the feelings off and headed to the small kitchen. I made me some hot chocolate and a fried egg.

I took my breakfast out to my verandah and sat there thinking about the night before, wondering if this was it or if we had a future together. . . .

Chapter Six

Gaza

Three months later . . .

"Yo, my nigga, I got word where the niggas stayed at that killed Ratty," Gio said as we sat at the bar, drinking.

"Oh word. Well, we need to get on it real quick, before they make another move."

"Yeah, there's this little bitch that I be fucking on the low low. She's friend with one of nigga's sister. The other night, after I finished fucking her and shit, I asked her if she didn't hear anything about Ratty's murder. At first, she was kind of hesitant to tell me anything, but I put on my charm, letting her know how much I want to be with her. Shortly after that, she started telling me that she heard some things. I continued pressing her, until she broke down and told me that she went to the bitch

name Sheena's house, and her brother, Markes,
and his crew was sitting around talking. She was
shocked when they started bragging about killing
Ratty. She said they were dapping each other up
and just drinking and smoking. I swear, when that
bitch was telling me this, my blood started boiling.
I wanted to pull my gun and hit that bitch, but I
didn't. I know in order to get them niggas, I might
need that bitch. So I kept my cool . . . Now I'm
ready to execute a plan."

"Yo, so these niggas stay in the Gully?" I asked
him.

"Yeah. I know the house that them niggas be at
and everything."

"Oh, word, so what we waiting on?"

"I just wanted to run this by you. I know some
of the niggas personally, and they ain't no soft-
ass niggas. They cold-blooded killers. If we goin'
to go in, we going to have to rush them or cut
them down one by one."

"Shit, it don't matter which way," I told him.
"Them pussy niggas need to die for what they did.
Fuck them niggas. We coming for them."

We sat there plotting how we were going to
approach these niggas. See, it was war time, and
we were going in heavy. . . .

***

"Yo, boss. I got word where the niggas are staying at for sure," Gio told me over the phone the next day.

"A'ight. Round up the niggas. We need a meeting ASAP. No time to waste. I'm on my way now." I made a few stops along the way to the bar, dropping off work to a few niggas that I had started fucking with.

The block that the bar sat on was quiet when I approached in my car: only a few people were walking or sitting out in their yard. I scoped out my surroundings before I pulled up to the back of the bar. Everything seemed straight. I checked my waist. Even though those people inside were my family, I still came prepared, since the niggas that had touched Ratty might be lurking around, hoping to catch their next victim slipping. I entered without warning. Niggas' voices could be heard blasting from the back room. When I walked into that room, everyone's attention turned to me.

"What's up, fellas?" I gave dap to each of them.

"Whaddup, boss?" they replied in unison.

"I'm here. I know Gio done informed y'all why we are here on such short notice. A while back, one of these niggas took out one of our soldiers, took him away from his family, his young children. That to me is straight violation. Some of y'all were ready to go to war, but I begged y'all not to. From past experience, I know if we went to war at the time, it would be detrimental to our clique and what we're trying to build. Not only would there be casualties, but we would also make ourselves hot, would have the police on our trail. Fast forward to today, and shit has died down, and the day is here when we will get revenge for Ratty's death."

I took a pause so I could look each man in the room in his eyes. I really was trying to see the expressions on their faces. In any clique, there was always a bitch nigga. I hadn't had the time to figure out who the bitch was in our clique.

I went on. "We gonna ride in two cars. We gonna be in and out. These niggas are part of the Get Money Crew, and from what I have learned, they are some vicious niggas. I'm trying to say, we ain't about to play no kind of games with them," I warned.

"So, how we gonna do this, boss?" Killa asked.

"Word is they be using the back entrance. It's a cut back there, so we gonna park beside the old house that is directly beside the crib. We gonna jump out of our cars and run directly to the back of the house. They only have two doors, the front and the back. Two niggas will stay in the car, just in case anyone runs out. And if they do, we will cut them down. Everybody in that house needs to go," I said, looking at my niggas.

I continued. "This has to be done. Before the day is over, their bitches, mothers, and whoever the fuck they're close to will be going up to Madden's to make funeral arrangements. A'ight, y'all ready?"

"Let's get it," Gio said. Then he jumped up and walked out of the back room.

We all split up and got in two cars. Me, Gio, and Leroy jumped in an old car that Gio drove in situations like this. My blood was pumping hard as excitement rushed over me. I remembered the days in New York when we went on operations like this. We were some killers, causing havoc all over the streets of New York, especially in the Bronx. When we got near our enemies' crib, I scoped out the front entrance and noted that the block was clear. We continued down the lane, toward the back of the house. It was our lucky day; the lane was clear. But this kind of made me nervous, since I'd never seen this lane without people out and about.

Leroy was going to be the one that stayed in the car, just in case any unwanted visitors popped up. I parked near the back of the house, quickly jumped out of the car, and sprinted through the alley to the back door, with Gio close on my heels. One of my soldiers, Trevor, was already at the door, and as soon as he saw me and Gio, he kicked the door in. It flew open, and we went in busting. They were on point, busting right back at us. We had masks over our faces, so I knew they were trying to figure out who the fuck we were.

I scoped out the nigga named Markes. I recognized him from a picture that Gio had shown me a few days ago. He was trying to get one of his niggas that had got hit out of the way. That nigga's eyes and mine locked. We started busting at one another. Markes's little gun was no match for the FN pistol that I was clutching. I ran down on the nigga, while trying to dodge the bullets he was busting. I hit him in the shoulder.

"Yo, pussy, you just shot me," he said as he tried firing back.

I removed my mask. "This is for my nigga Ratty," I said before I put half of my clip into his body. His lifeless body dropped to the floor, and I stood over him and fired one straight to his dome.

A split second later I heard a string of shots ring out. I ducked behind the couch and tried to analyze the situation. The gunfire ceased for a second, then started back up again. I ran in the direction that it was coming from. I spot my niggas Killa and Trevor pulling a body, so I dashed over to them. I looked down and stopped dead in my tracks, thinking it was a dream. But it wasn't. My nigga Gio, my right-hand, my motherfucking brother, was the one they were pulling. Gio's bullet-riddled body was spread across the floor, and I saw that he had taken a couple of slugs to the chest. Blood gushed out of his wounds.

"Yo, what the fuck happened?" I yelled, signaling with my hand for them to stop pulling Gio. I got down on my knees, dropped my gun, and checked his pulse. There wasn't one. "Yo, we need to get him out of here fast. Help me get him to the car. Hang on, Gio. I got you bro. Hang on."

We picked him up and ran through the back door and to the car, where Leroy was waiting. We placed Gio on the backseat, and then me and Killa squeezed in next to him, while Trevor hopped in the front passenger seat.

"Yo, let's go! Gio got to get to the hospital!" I shouted at Leroy.

Leroy pulled off and headed in the direction of the hospital.

"Hang on, Gio. Bro, we got shit to do. You can't go nowhere, bro," I kept saying. In my heart I was begging God to save my nigga's life. The fucking traffic was horrible, which made it impossible to get to the fucking hospital quickly.

I knew before we even got there, my nigga was gone. Not a single sound was coming from him. I felt sick. I buried my head in my hands. I couldn't think straight right now. . . .

Twenty minutes later Leroy finally pulled up to the entrance of Kingston Public Hospital.

"Yo, pull to the side," I said sadly. "He is dead. I'ma try to get him in this hospital real quick. Then I'ma run back out. We can't stick around. Have too much guns and shit up in here."

Leroy pulled over to the side so other cars could get by us. Then I dragged Gio's body out of the car. A security guard spotted me and rushed over.

"Yo, help me get him in there," I said.

He radioed for help. Soon as he did that, I looked around, then walked over to the car door.

"Yo, where you going? They going to talk to you," the security guard yelled.

I wasn't trying to hear that shit. My knees were wobbly, and I felt nauseated. But I needed to get the fuck up out of here.

"C'mon, Father. Get in. We got to go right now," Leroy demanded.

I took one last look at Gio. My heart was telling me to go be with my brother, but my mind was letting me know I needed to get the fuck up out of here. The way the system was fucked up, these guards would hold on to me, like I was the one that did this. I climbed in the backseat, and Leroy sped off into traffic.

"Yo, Father, this one hit hard. That's our family man," Leroy said to me, his voice trembling. I knew he was hurting too.

I let Leroy take me to the crib after he drove Killa and Trevor back to the bar. I needed a minute to get my mind straight. Camille was still at the crib when I got there. She came outside when Leroy and I got out of the car. She just looked at me. The tears were rolling down my face. I couldn't even hold them in anymore.

"What's wrong, babe?" she inquired.

"Ma, he's gone. He's dead," I said before collapsing on the driveway.

"Who is dead? Leroy, what he talking about?"

"Gio dead, Camille."

"Are you okay, babes?" she said as she kneeled down next to me. "Leroy, help me get him inside and put him on the couch."

I staggered to my feet, and they helped me to walk inside the house and get to the couch. I couldn't think straight at all. All I could see was Gio's dead body on the ground. I knew shit was going to get sticky in the Gully, so before I closed my eyes on that couch, I told Camille to stay at the house tonight, without letting her know what was going to take place.

It was nightfall before I awoke and opened my eyes again. Leroy was sitting close by, smoking a blunt, and Camille was sitting beside me.

"Here, baby. Drink this." She handed me a cup.

I took a sip. It was Patrón. I needed this. I was hoping I would wake up from this nightmare, but seeing Leroy made me replay everything that had happened earlier, and I knew it wasn't no dream. My nigga really was gone. From New York to prison, back to Jamaica, we had stayed in touch. We had had plans to make millions together and to take over this country. . . . Where the fuck was I at when a nigga shot up my brother? Anger turned into guilt. Where the fuck was I at . . . ?

"Nah, Ma, I need sump'n stronger. Bring me a bottle of vodka and roll me up a couple blunts," I instructed Camille.

She appeared with the vodka in no time. As I downed the liquor, it burned my throat, but I really didn't give a fuck. My heart was crushed. My boy, my right-hand, my brother was gone. Probably laid up on ice, all alone in the morgue. Who was going to watch my back? Life was never going to be the same.

"Camille, my brother is gone, Ma." Tears rolled down my face. I was a nigga who didn't cry, but my soul had been ripped into pieces with this one. Just yesterday Gio and I were eating, drinking, and talking shit together. Just like that, this nigga was gone.

"Baby, he's in a better place."

"Yeah, yeah. God should've took me instead, B. Gio didn't deserve that shit. He was a good youth. His family was depending on him."

"Yeah, you right, but Gio was a thorough nigga, and he know what these streets were about. I don't know what happen, but I just know God don't make no mistake."

Leroy came over to me. "Here, my nigga. Here go a big head. Camille, bring some more liquor out here. This is some fucked-up shit. Gaza need to drink and drown out this pain."

Before the night was over, I finished that bottle of vodka and two bottles of Patrón. When that didn't drown out my pain anymore, I started on the Jamaican white rum and smoked about five blunts. Leroy and I sat out on the verandah, most of the time just quiet. When we did talk, we only shared memories of the shit Gio did to help both of us. This nigga was a real one, and I swore that God didn't even make them like this no more. It had been a while since I got pissy drunk, but I had to block out the entire day's events. Tomorrow was going to be a much rougher day,

I knew, since reality would set in and I would have to face everyone. . . .

The next day I could barely raise my head up. I was so fucked up that when I stood up, I staggered a little. Camille helped me walk from the bed to the living-room couch. After I sat down, she headed into the kitchen.

"Gaza, here go a cup of tea. It will help you a little," Camille said when she returned to the living room. "I talk to my girl, and she said the whole Gully are mourning Gio death. She also said about seven niggas from round First Street was found dead. She said police is everywhere. They talking about doing a curfew until they can get this killing under control."

I really didn't say anything. I liked Camille and everything, but I wasn't the nigga to start telling no bitch that I was just fucking some shit that could land me in prison.

Leroy walked up just then. "Father, how you holding up?"

"Hmm, I can't even answer that, my nigga. Right now I'm numb. I ain't got no feelings right now." I took a sip of the tea Camille had made me.

"Hey, boo, I'ma run some errand," Camille interjected. "I call a taxi. I'll come back to check on you later. I'll call you first."

"A'ight, babes."

After Camille's cab came and she left, Leroy took a seat across from me.

"Aye, Father, something is on my mind, and I can't figure it out."

"Whaddup?" I looked at him. I could tell he was worried about something.

"Father, I could be wrong still, but something seems off. I mean, Gio was a soldier, and he was on point. So how did them niggas catch him slipping? Plus, Gio always wear a vest. How did he die so easy? Maybe I'm tripping, but this shit don't make sense to me, mon."

I sat there quietly, thinking about everything that he was saying to me. I looked at him. He was dead-ass serious. . . . Shit was crazy. I did know Gio wore a vest. He had even given me the one I had. I was confused about how Gio had got shot, but I knew he was shot in the head. Only a nigga that was aware that Gio was wearing a vest would make sure to shoot him in the head. Now that Leroy had brought this to my attention, he had me thinking.

"Yo, what do you think happen?" I was eager to find out what he was thinking.

"I don't really know. I was in the car at the time. I just don't see how Gio got shot up like that. Who was supposed to be watching his back? Who was around him?"

Leroy was raising some valid points, but I had no answers. I knew where I had been at when Gio got shot, but I had no idea where everyone else had been at. This had me thinking, though.

"Hmm, you know, now that you bring this up, I'ma get to the bottom of it. I just want to know what the fuck happen in that room," I said.

"Father, I don't want to put no nigga out there without proof, but that nigga Killa is suspect. A few weeks ago, him and Gio had a little beef. I'm not sure if he mention it to you or not. But we were down by the bar when Gio mention some money was missing. He went off, and Killa took offense, talking about he didn't like how Gio was talking like he was dissing niggas. Gio pulled his gun and pointed it at the nigga head and ask if he was ready to die. Killa backed down, but everybody know shit wasn't the same after that day. Killa the type of nigga that takes no disrespect from no one."

I sat there smoking and drinking the tea while I listened to what Leroy was saying to me. Damn, Gio was my right-hand. Why the fuck did I not know this? My nigga had fucked up. The rule in the streets was, if you pulled a burner on a nigga, you had to out the nigga. You couldn't turn your back on that nigga, 'cause he was going to always remember that you punked him, and that you did it front of other niggas. . . . I shook my head in disgust. This shit was fucking crazy. Could it be that one of our niggas outed my nigga?

"Yo, Leroy, on my life, I hope this little nigga ain't got shit to do with my nigga's death."

"Boss, if I didn't feel it in my soul, I wouldn't even have brought it to you. But ever since you told me what happened, that shit is just sitting on my mind. I really hope I'm wrong, but, shit, niggas are so grimy nowadays that you can't trust even the niggas that you roll with."

"Trust me, my nigga, I know. Remember that's how me and Gio them catch our case. The nigga that I broke bread with was feeding the Feds information. I ain't goin' to lie. The day my lawyer told me Demari was snitching, I almost broke down and cry. I took this nigga out the streets, put him on. Shit, took that nigga around my family and treat him like family. That shit cut me deep, yo."

Leroy nodded. "Yo, I don't trust no bloodclaat man or bitch. I done see certain bwoy turned against their brethren for a few hundred dollars. This gamed is cutthroat and deadly. That's why

I keep this pistol by my side at all times, even when I'm taking a shit. I'll knock a nigga wig off without hesitation. Gio was a good youth. He took me from Grants Pen and put me on with his team so I could start making a few dollars. I'll forever be grateful to him, 'cause if it was not for him, I wouldn't be able to send the youth them to school or pay fi food on the table on the regular. Trust me, that's a real nigga." He started tearing up.

"Yo, you ain't got to tell me. I been dealing with that nigga for over fifteen years, and that's real nigga. Straight forward, what you see is what you get from him. This shit ain't fair . . ." My words trailed off.

My eyes were tearing up. This shit was hard as fuck. People were hitting up my phone, but I cut it off after ignoring them. I really didn't know what to say, and every time somebody say RIP, my heart ached. All the niggas were dead, so there was no one left to kill to avenge my nigga's death, but if I found out those dead ones were not responsible for my nigga's death and Killa was, this little nigga was going to pay dearly. . . .

Just the thought of a nigga on our team doing this aroused anger in me. I wanted to just wild out, but I knew Gio wouldn't want me to just act out. I smiled as I remembered the night he handed me the key fob to the BMW. My nigga was a real one. . . .

I went through Red Hills and dropped some money off to Gio's peoples. His mother and them had just flown down from Connecticut. I was trying not to see them, but there was no escaping it. This was my nigga, and everybody knew how close we were.

"Hello, Miss Ivy," I said as I removed my Cazal shades as I stood on the verandah.

"I know you. Hold on . . . Donavan."

"Yes, ma'am. It's me."

"Donavon, what happen to my son?"

"Miss Ivy, I don't even know, but trust me, I'm trying to find out."

"Donavan, I remember how tight you and Gio was back in New York. If you see one, you see the next. Well, these animals took him from us. They took my baby, Donavan. They cut him down like an animal," she said, fighting back the tears.

It was one of the hardest things for me to do, stand there listening to his mother's pain. I reached over and grabbed her in a tight hug.

"Donavan, please find whoever did this to my son. Find them and make sure that's the last breath they took. That's only way my baby will rest and I will get some comfort." Her words were cold.

"I got you, Miss Ivy. I promise, I got you," I assured her.

We hugged a little while longer, until someone walked out on the verandah.

"Miss Ivy, I'm about to bounce. Here is a million dollars. Take it and pay for his funeral. I'll be back through to drop off some more soon," I said. I shoved a bag in her hand. She looked at me, looked at the bag, and start crying.

"I love you, Donavan. I always told my son, you was a real one."

"Love you too, Miss Ivy. I got to go now."

I couldn't stick around. My heart was breaking, and I was trying my hardest not to break down in front of these people. I threw my shades on, left the verandah, and walked out of the yard with my head hanging low. I didn't bother to acknowledge the people that were crowded around the gate. I jumped in my car and pulled off. This shit was sad. It had been days since Gio died, and the pain hadn't seemed to ease up none. As I drove, I lit up the blunt that I had rolled earlier. I wanted to roll through the Gully, but the police was out in full force. They had imposed a curfew in the area: no one could be out on the streets after 7:00

p.m. The murders that had taken place was all over the news. People were protesting and asking the police commissioner to do something about bringing the killers in to face justice. It was best that I continued to lay low for about another week. That was all I could do. Soon as shit cleared up, I was going to go in and clean the place up. I didn't trust anyone, and I would hate for Babylon to run up in there. I got so much work ready to be shipped off overseas.

Chapter Seven

Camille

I hated to see Gaza hurting like this, but what could I do? I knew him and Gio was best friends, and he was taking his death pretty hard. I'd tried to comfort him in every way that I could, but one second he was doing okay and the next second he was sitting there, sad, and just reminiscing about all the good times they had had in New York. I'd known Gio my entire life, and I was hurting too. I mean, that nigga was a good dude. In our community, ain't really nobody had anything bad to say about him, and if they did, it was because they had violated him. He was a don and made sure the kids had stuff for school. If anything happened, he was the first one they called. Who the fuck were we supposed to call on now? My eyes watered up as I thought about Gio. We used to sit in the bar late at night, laughing and talking. Never knew the end was this close.

Damn, Gio, my linky, my genna, rest up. . . .

I grabbed my bags. I was going to go see Gaza and spend the night with him. Lately, we had been spending a lot of time together. I wasn't sure where we were heading, but I did know I was falling in love with him, deep and fast. Just the other day, I'd been ignoring him, playing hard to get, and now look at me. That nigga had me wide open.

I looked at the time. It was about to be curfew time, so I needed to hurry up and get from around here. I welcomed the curfew because of all the killings that had taken place. I stepped outside, locked the grill, and walked out of the yard. I waved to a few people as I headed up the street. As I walked up the lane, I glanced over my shoulder and saw two dudes walking fast behind me. I tried to ignore them and continued about my business. However, I felt their footsteps getting closer behind me. I started to walk a little faster. I thought about running, but I was probably tripping, so I just continued on at a walk. I was almost to the main road, where the taxis were, when I felt something being pressed hard against my back, and then someone grabbed me and covered my mouth.

"You Camille, right? Don't say a word. Just shake yo' head," a male voice said to me.

I shook my head yes. I didn't know how the fuck . . . I just knew there was a gun or another hard object pressing into my back. I started saying a silent prayer, asking God not to let these niggas rape me.

"Bitch, we heard you fucking with Yankee bwoy Gaza, and we know he got something to do with the killing around here," the same male voice said. "So we want you to deliver a message for us. Tell that pussy, we coming for him and everybody associated with him."

The dude who had grabbed me and had spoken removed his hand from my mouth. He let me go and stepped in front of me, pointed the gun in my face as his accomplice looked on. "This is not a joke. The next time we see you with that nigga, yo' bloodclaat mother will be visiting you in the morgue." He grinned in my face, revealing his dirty set of rotten teeth.

"Come out of my bloodclaat face, dutty bwoy," I snarled as I took a good look at them.

"Bitch, this is a warning. Next time, we won't be so friendly." He kept the gun aimed at my face and pretended that he was shooting it.

My body shivered as I thought that this was my final moment. But without saying another word, the two of them ran off down a side road, where zincs were used to separate houses. I stood there for a few seconds. I was trying to decide if I should go back home or go on about my business. I didn't recognize the nigga that had made the threats, but the other one's face was familiar. I just couldn't place it, though. I looked at the time. I had a few minutes to go before the task force rode in. I started walking fast to get to the taxis. . . .

I was still trembling hard as hell when I got into a taxi five minutes later. I had lived here my entire life and had never experienced no kind of shit like this. These niggas were bold as fuck, running up on me like that. . . .

I got to Gaza's house, paid the driver, and got out of the taxi. The house was dark when I got there, but I saw his car, so I knew he was inside. I dialed his number and waited. I wouldn't dare go inside the gate, even though he had given me the code. Just last week he had bought two big-ass German sheperd dogs. He said it was extra security, but I was scared out of my mind. Soon as they spotted me at the gate, they came rushing over, barking.

"Yo, what a gwaan, babes?" Gaza said when he answered his phone.

"I'm at the gate, you know. But these dogs are acting a fool."

"All right. Give me a second. Just coming out the shower."

"Okay."

Even though I was no longer in the ghetto, I kept looking around to see if anyone had followed me. I was still shaking from the incident earlier. A few minutes later, Gaza walked out of the house in only his shorts, revealing his toned chest. I knew this wasn't the time to be looking at how sexy this man was, but I couldn't help it.

"What's up, babes?"

I didn't answer him. I hurried to the verandah and took a seat.

"Yo, you good?" he said when he reached the verandah.

"Some bwoy just hold me up."

"What you mean? Them rob you?" He looked at me, obviously confused.

"Nah. I'm walking toward Fourth Avenue to catch a taxi to come check you. I see two dudes behind me, so I start to walk up, because it was getting a little dark. Them run down on me and put a gun in my back—"

"What the fuck they said?" he asked, cutting me off.

"One of the bwoy tell me to tell you, them know is you that kill the people them the other day, and they coming for you and everybody that you love."

"Oh word! Niggas sending message to me. Did you recognize the pussy them?" He started pacing.

"Nah. Not the one that put the gun on me, but he knew my name. The other one didn't say too much, but I've seen him before. I just need to think where the fuck I know him from."

"Yo, these pussyhole them playing a deadly game. No nigga can't threaten my life and live to brag about it. I been cooling, but I see niggas want war," he yelled out.

"Gaza, did you have anything to do with the murder them?"

"Baby girl, I done told you, I know nothing about that shit."

I looked at him and could tell he was lying. I knew him and Gio had been plotting to go after whoever had killed Ratty. Rumor had it, it was the niggas that got killed who had killed Ratty. I had a feeling Gaza wasn't going to be honest with me, so I dropped the subject.

"Yo, it's not safe for you to continue living down by the Gully," he said, breaking the silence.

"What you mean? This is my home. I don't have nowhere to go. Can't go by my mother and them house, because they don't have no space. Plus, I'm a big woman. I'm not going to catch at nobody's house," I hissed.

I was getting aggravated because I didn't know what the fuck had gone down. I had nothing to do with this shit, and now I had been thrown into it.

"Listen, baby. These niggas know you fuck with me, which makes you a target. I already lose a brother. I can't risk losing my bitch too. Pack up your stuff tomorrow, and I'll get a few niggas to move you up here with me."

"Yo, I never live with a man before, so I don't know."

"Yo, Camille, it's not up for debate. In order to keep you alive, I need you to be here, where I can protect you. I can't protect you if you down there."

I looked at this nigga, and he was serious as a heart attack. He really was acting like he ran me and I didn't have no say-so. I wasn't feeling this at all. I got up, walked inside the house, headed into the bedroom, and lay down. I really didn't feel like talking, because all this shit was moving too fast for me.

The next morning my phone started ringing, which woke me up. I looked over at the other side of the bed. I noticed it hadn't been slept in. That meant Gaza hadn't come into the bedroom last night. This irritated me. I looked at the time; it was a little after 8:00 a.m. I got up, went into the bathroom to brush my teeth and wash my face. Then I wandered out of the bathroom and saw that the front door was open, so I walked out to the verandah. Gaza was standing by the grill, dressed in all black from head to toe. This was strange, 'cause Kingston weather wasn't no joke. I knew his ass was burning up.

"You didn't sleep here last night?" I quizzed.

"Nah. I had some business to handle," he responded, sounding slightly irritated.

"*Business*? Do you mean another bitch?" I hated to go there with him, because our relationship was still new and I didn't want to come off as being insecure.

"Yo, you tripping, B. Look at all the crazy shit taking place in my life, and you think a nigga is worried about a bitch? Yo, you need to get your mind right."

"All I did was ask a question. Why the fuck you invite me up here, and you know you were leaving? For all this, I could've stayed home."

He looked at me, shook his head, then spoke. "This is your home now. So get used to being home by yourself sometimes. I'm a businessman. I got moves to make in these streets and money to make. I don't always have time to lay up in the bed and hold you. If that's what you're looking for, then you're looking for the wrong shit. I'm a boss, so my bitch got to be a boss too and understand there are times when she got to hold shit down . . ." With that, he walked through the gate, jumped in his car, and pulled off.

I stood there with my mouth wide open. . . . This bwoy was really cutting up. Tears gathered in my eyes. I was feeling confused and hurt. I mean, weeks ago, he was asking me to be his girl, and now that he had got the pussy, he was coming at me all aggressive and shit. . . . What the fuck was I supposed to do? I didn't feel safe living in the Gully, all because of him, and living here with him ain't starting off too good. I took a seat on the sofa on the verandah and just let the tears flow freely. . . .

Chapter Eight

Gaza

They say time heals all wounds, but I doubted if my wounds would ever be healed. My nigga was gone behind some nonsense, and here I was, having to run this shit by myself. Business was stalled while all this shit was going on. But I woke up this morning, and I remembered the motto that Gio had lived by. "If it don't make money, it don't make sense." With that said, I jumped out of the bed, took a quick shower, and got dressed. Then I stood on my balcony, smoking a blunt and plotting out my next move.

"Here you go, babes. A cup of your favorite," Camille said as she stepped out on the balcony. She handed me a cup of coffee.

"Thanks, beautiful. You know exactly what your man needs." I reached over and kissed her on her forehead.

"I try."

"Aye, Camille, have you considered what your next move is going to be?"

"Uh, no. I mean, I was going to see if I could do some more dance competitions. So I can make some more money and maybe get on with one of these big deejays."

"I hear you. Well, I got some moves that you might be interested in. You can make a whole lot of money."

She looked at me in a suspicious manner and said nothing.

"Don't worry about it now," I told her. "I got to figure out everything, but we can get rich together, babes. Trust me."

"All right. Just let me know."

I knew she may not be down at first, but I had the power to manipulate any situation. Just then I heard my phone ringing, so I took it out of my pocket.

"Yo."

"Gaza, what's up, son? You a hard man to catch up with."

"What's good, Rio? Just been cooling after all this shit that went down with Gio and shit. Things got a little sticky, so I been trying to lay low."

"Again, my sincere condolences, but Gio is among the dead, and we're still here. And business can't wait no longer. My people been hitting me up from left to right. I've been giving them the runaround 'cause I been waiting to hear from you. So tell me something good, my nigga."

"My apologies, Rio, but I can get something to you by Friday, no later than Sunday."

"Sounds good, sounds good. Same price?"

"Yeah, well, it depends on what you trying to get."

"I need a whole shipment. About eighty kil is good."

"A'ight," I said slowly. "I don't know if I can pull that much right now. Let me get some things in motion, and I will get back with you ASAP."

"A'ight, son. I'll be waiting."

Shit! If I could pull off this shipment without it getting seized, I could make close to a hundred million dollars. This would be the biggest lick for us, and it definitely would put me in a great spot right now.

I needed to get on this right now. I pulled up my nigga's number. This nigga was my and Gio's partner in this. He was a really laid-back nigga who barely ever showed his face. He had a big mansion up by Beverly Hills, and Gio had told me, he was very careful about who he did business with. I dialed the number.

"Hello."

"Yo, boss man. I need to come visit you," I said.

"I gotcha, and please come by yourself and make sure no stray dogs follow you in."

"No worries. I'm on my way," I told him, and we ended the call.

I walked downstairs and stepped into the kitchen. It was smelling good.

"What are you cooking, babes?"

Camille looked over at me from her place at the stove. "Some curry chicken back, with dumpling and banana. I figured you was hungry."

"That I am, but I got an important run to go make."

"C'mon, Gaza. The food almost finished," she pouted.

"Trust me, babes, I wish I could just eat right now, but I have something to handle that will change our lives forever. So no, it can't wait. I'll be back soon, though."

I grabbed my keys from the kitchen counter and left out. Then I hopped behind the wheel of my car.

All the way to Beverly Hills, my mind was racing. This was a big order, but I had faith that we could pull it off. I made sure the coast was clear before I pulled up at the Big Man's mansion. Everything seemed cool, so I approached the gates, came to a stop, and pressed the intercom button.

"How may I help you?" a female voice yelled.

"It's Gaza. I'm here to see the boss."

The electric gates started opening, and when they were finished, I drove in and the gates immediately closed behind me. This was my second time coming up here, and I felt the same way now as I had felt the last time. Like this was prison. The walls around the house were high, and the tops were covered with barbed wire. The minute you entered the property, around four guard dogs made their presence known. And it seemed as if cameras were on every inch of the property.

I drove closer to the house, then stopped and sat in my car, the engine still running, and waited for one of the many houseboys to come out and get me. I wouldn't dare exit my car with all these fucking dogs looking for their next piece of fresh meat. A few minutes later, someone exited the mansion and walked up to my car. He motioned for me to put my window down.

"Yo, is you name Gaza?" he asked.

"Yeah."

"Follow me. The boss man is waiting for you."

I cut the car off, got out, and followed him. He said some shit to the dogs as they ran toward us, and they obeyed and went back over to the side of the house. He then opened the front door, and we stepped into the foyer. I caught sight of a few bitches, who were either half naked or had on minimal clothing. They waved to me and smiled. These were some bad-ass bitches, especially that little Asian-looking one. I would love to fuck her. . . .

"The boss man up there, on the back patio." The houseboy pointed to the stairs.

I walked up the stairs and was about to step out on the back patio when a big, bulky security-looking dude stepped in front me. "Hand me your gun."

"What the fuck you need my gun for?"

"No one talks to the boss with a weapon on them."

I looked at this nigga and shook my head. I then reached in my waist, pulled out my gun, and gave it to him.

"The boss man is waiting on you." This bitch-ass nigga smiled at me.

I was seconds away from swinging on his bitch ass, but I was here to handle important business, so I controlled myself. Plus, I already knew he was only taking orders. I stepped out on the patio.

"Gaza, my man, welcome to my house," the boss man said without turning around.

"Bless up, Father."

I went to stand beside him at a wall that over-looked the entire city. I thought the view at my crib was dope. This was way better. You could stand here and see vehicles coming from miles away. If you were into illegal activities, this was definitely the view you needed.

The boss man caught my eye. "I heard what happen to Gio. I sent my condolences. Did you handle it?"

"Yeah, it's handled. Everything good."

"Are you sure? Because you can't do good business if there is a war going on."

"Trust me, I know. That was one of the reasons why I've been laying low for a while, but my America people are hungry for that work."

He nodded. "Talk to me. What can I do to help you?"

"Well, Father, I know you and Gio had a deal that was working for y'all, and I respect it, but Gio is gone and I'm the one that will be running this organization. With that said, I want us to be partners . . ."

"Partners? Ha-ha. And why do you think I would need a partner? And what makes you qualified?"

"What makes me qualified is the fact that while I might be fresh in Jamaica, I am not in America. Niggas know me, and they respect my business, from Miami to New York to Boston. Yes, you have the supply of coke, but you don't have the market to move it swiftly. You can definitely use the help to get the product shipped off, up to one hundred kil at a time. Together, I feel like we can have the coke game on lock."

He said nothing at first. Just gazed out at the view, deep in thought. We stood there in complete silence for over three minutes.

"Hmm, you sound like every other nigga that is dreaming of taking over this drug game," he said finally. "I don't mean no disrespect, but you were just deported. The Feds could still be hot on your ass. Doing business with you could be risky."

"Doing business with *anyone* can be risky," I returned. "I'm a real nigga. I know how to handle business. I can even go in with half of the money to show you I'm about my business. No disrespect, if you don't want to fuck with me, 'cause I got deported, let me know so I can go find someone that wants to get on board with me. Time is money, and I got moves to make. My New York people are expecting a shipment no later than Sunday. That give me only around five days to get things done."

"You know, Gaza, I love your drive. Matter of fact, you remind me of myself around twenty years ago. Young, ambitious, and hungry. We can definitely do business, but I will deal only with you, and with no one else. These niggas in this country are greedy, and greed creates envy, which can become deadly. In this game, no one can be trusted, and I mean no one outside of yourself. You can't even trust the bitch you laid up with at night, 'cause I've learned they will betray you for the next nigga that has more money . . ."

He was spitting some real shit, but I was no stranger to the game, so these were all things that I already knew or practiced.

"So do we have a deal?" I asked him.

"We got a deal."

We exchanged daps and sealed the deal with a glass of Grey Goose. We sat on the balcony, playing with the numbers and making sure we were making the best deal possible. I loved how he did his business: he didn't get his hands dirty with anything. Before I left, he introduced me to two of his most loyal men, who would be working with me.

While I was glad I would be doing business with the boss man, I was happy when I drove off that day and was no longer behind the gates, the walls, and the barbed wire of that mansion. I didn't like anything that reminded me of prison. But I was convinced that forming this partnership was the right move, because I would be able to handle my business now.

Chapter Nine

Camille

Gaza had my mind all over the place. I was still thinking on what the hell he was talking about when he said he had a way for us to make money. I mean, I was hungry and was looking for ways to make money, but I wasn't into doing no drug shit, and I knew that this was what they were in. I had done watched too many shows and heard too many horror stories of bitches who got caught up in the drug thing because of their niggas. There were two things that I had said I would never get involved in, and they were selling pussy and transporting drugs. Both those things could have you either dead or doing life in prison. And me, I loved my life and my freedom too much to risk it.

This was the day that Gaza was having the dudes move my stuff out of my place. My landlord had been shocked when I told his ass I was leaving his place. He had tried talking me out of it, but my mind was made up. Shit, if you asked me, his ass had been getting one over on me. This little-ass apartment wasn't worth no twenty-five grand per month, but I was grateful that I had had a roof over my head, so I didn't complain.

I didn't have much to move. I had only my bedroom set, which I'd bought when I first moved in, and my couch, which I had decided to give to Sophia. Speaking of Sophia, why her ass ain't at the house? I had told her what time I was coming around here. I pulled her number up now and dialed.

"Hello?" she said when she answered.

"I thought you was coming to get the settee before I leave out?"

"Oh shit! I didn't know you was up there. I'ma tell Oneil to come grab it, and I'm on my way."

"All right," I said before I hung up.

The dudes packed the bedroom set and the suitcases containing my clothes in a small truck and then left. I grabbed a broom, mop, and bucket and started to clean the house. My landlord didn't give me his place dirty, so I didn't want to leave it without cleaning it.

"Gyal, I can't believe you leaving me," Sophia said as she stepped up on the verandah.

"Goody, I done explain to you, so the thing set. But guess what? It don't matter where I live. You still my best friend, and we still going to hang out and part together."

"I know, but it's not the same. We have been only houses apart. Now I'm still in the Gully, and you're uptown, living the good life. I'm happy for you still. Just wish I was going with you."

I looked her right in the eye. "Listen, you're my ride-and-die bitch, and that will never change. No other gyal can take your place. I'm just a phone call away, and soon as I get settled in, you will be coming to see me."

"You right about that. I love you, bitch."

"Love you too. Now move. Let me finish cleaning this man place before him come get his key."

"Fuck that slumlord. Him bloodclaat lucky it's not me who's moving, 'cause I would leave this piece of shit just like this."

"You too wicked, man." I burst out laughing.

We continued talking until her man came and got the couch. We hugged, and she left. As soon as I was left alone, I began to feel nervous, so I hurried up and finished what I was doing. The voice of that nigga who had stuck a gun in my back echoed in my head. Once I was done cleaning the place, I waited twenty minutes to see if the landlord was coming, but he didn't show up. I called his phone and got no response. *Oh well*, I thought. I didn't intend to stick around not one second longer, so I grabbed my purse, took one last look around. I was stepping out the door when I heard voices outside the apartment. I turned my head to look.

"There go the gyal!" I heard a voice say. I recognized it as the voice of the nigga who had grabbed me that evening and threatened me.

I knew this situation wasn't good, so I turned to run. . . .

Pop! Pop! Pop!

I tried to get away, but my feet were not fast enough. I felt something hit my bag, and I tried to run faster. Then something sharp hit my leg, and I went down. . . .

"Jesus Christ! Y'all try to kill the gyal!" I heard my landlord shout.

I heard more gunshots ring out, and then it was quiet.

"Call the police," I heard voices say in unison.

I knew I was going to die, so I started to cry and pray. I was scared of dying and definitely didn't want to die like this. I was in so much pain. . . . I tried to stay awake, but I was so sleepy. . . .

***

"Can you hear me?" I heard a voice ask.

I slowly opened my eyes and looked around. I could tell I was in the hospital, but I couldn't move. I had wires strung up all over my body. I couldn't move my leg.

"I'm happy you are awake, Miss Brown. I'm Dr. Lewis. Somebody did a number on your body, and for a minute there, we thought we had lost you. You're a strong young lady, and you fought your way back to us."

Hearing this man talk like that brought tears to my eyes, because when I was lying in that yard, I really thought I was going to die.

He went on. "You're in serious condition. The bullet that hit your back missed your spine by a few inches. We were able to remove it. The other bullet hit your leg, but this is only flesh wound. That one will heal up pretty fast if you stay off the leg and let it heal. This is the second day, and you're doing pretty good. Your vitals are great, and you're pretty stable."

"Thank you, Doctor."

"You're welcome. Oh, the police are waiting to see you."

"Okay. Thanks, Doctor."

After he left the room, two uniformed policemen entered.

"Miss Brown, how are you feeling?" one of them said.

I didn't respond, because this was a stupid-ass question. I had almost lost my life, and here they were, asking me dumb-ass questions, about how I was feeling.

The officer who had asked the question spoke again. "I'm Lieutenant Wilson, and this is Sergeant Davis. We are here concerning your injuries and assault. Is there anything you can tell us? Who did this to you?"

I had to think hard and long. Did I really want to tell the police who had done this? I had been raised never to talk to or trust the police. I had been raised in the Gully, and the only times I'd seen the police there were when they were attacking us or coming through, trying to intimidate us. So my motto was, "Fuck the police." It was crazy that here they were, standing in front of me, pretending like they gave a fuck.

I finally spoke. "I heard voices. I didn't recognize the voices. And I didn't see the people they belonged to."

"Are you sure? These ruthless thugs murdered an innocent man. I believe it's your landlord, Mr. Leonard. They almost killed you," Lieutenant Wilson said. "If you can think of anything to help us to bring them to justice, please tell us."

Hearing that Mr. Leonard had lost his life behind trying to help me brought tears to my eyes. This wasn't fair. . . .

"Like I told you a few minutes ago, I didn't see them. Maybe you can talk to the other people in the yard. They might've seen something."

"Miss Brown, do you know a Mr. Coley?" Sargeant Davis asked me.

"No. Why? Who is he?" I pretended like I was lost.

The sergeant stared at me. "That's strange, because I've talked to quite a few people who told me that you're the girlfriend of Mr. Coley. His name is also mentioned in reports of the shootings of several victims in the area. Your shooting is described as a revenge shooting. Someone getting at you to send a very important message to your boyfriend."

"No disrespect, but I done told y'all, I don't know no Mr. Coley. I'm single, so I don't know why people lying, talking about I got a boyfriend. Listen, I'm tired. Why don't y'all go back to whoever feeding y'all these lies?"

I closed my eyes. This was my sign to them that this conversation was over. I was tired, and my body was in pain.

"Okay, Miss Brown. If you remember anything, please don't hesitate to have the doctor or one of the nurses call the station," Lieutenant Wilson told me.

I didn't respond; I kept my eyes closed. I waited until the door had closed before I opened my eyes. But then I saw the door opening, and I was sure it was these fucking policemen again. I was ready to cuss them out. But then I saw my mama walk through the door.

"Mama!" I said as tears flooded my eyes. I hadn't seen my mama in weeks, not since the last time I visited her.

"Baby, how you feeling?" she said as she stood next to the bed and gazed down at me.

"In a lot of pain," I confessed.

"I was up here all yesterday. The minute I get the call, I rush up here and been here ever since. My phone was off, so I run to go pay it over Digicel. Baby, which pussy them do this to you?"

"Mama, I don't even know. I don't walk and mess with people, and I don't deserve this. Mama, I thought I was dead. All I could think about was how you was going to hurt."

"Baby, on my way up here, I pray and I pray. When I got up here and the doctor them tell how the boy them shot you up, I went in the bathroom up here, and I drop to my knees and I pray. I plead the blood of Jesus over you. I gave God the glory, and I knew then he was going to pull you through. You is my child, and you is a fighter, just like you mother."

"Mama, I'm in so much pain," I cried.

"I know, baby. Let me see if the nurse can get you something for that pain." She rubbed my head.

Before she could leave the room, Gaza walked in. Mama turned around and looked at him strangely.

"Who are you?" she said.

"Mama, this is Gaza, the guy that I was telling you about."

"This is the bwoy that the people them say get you mix up in all this?"

"Mama, stop. You don't know what you talking about, and they are only spreading lies."

She shook her head. "Hmm, you better wake up, baby girl. Don't make your heart write you a check that you can't cash."

I swear this lady, my mama, was pissing me the fuck off, and there was nothing I could do about it.

"Aye, Camille, this is your moms, and she has every right to feel how she feels," Gaza interjected. "I'm going to leave."

"No, you don't need to leave!" I exclaimed. "Mama was on her way out to get some pain medicine from the nurses' station. Right, Mama?"

She shot me a look, but she saw on my face that I wasn't playing. She walked out of the room.

Gaza walked closer to the bed. "Yo, hey, babes. How you feeling?"

"I'm here, boo."

"Yo, babes, listen, I don't want you to worry about nothing outside of getting better. I got you. Just know that . . . ," he said as he looked in my eyes.

I knew he was dead-ass serious, because I heard it in his voice.

"Babes, the police was here earlier," I told him.

"Yeah? What they wanted?"

"Wanted me to tell them who shot me . . . but that's not what bother me. What bother me is they know your name and were saying you had some shit to do with the shooting in the Gully. Them pussyhole people down by the Gully keep running their fucking mouth." I started to cough.

He sighed. "Didn't I just tell you to relax? I got you, babes. Focus on your health."

He was so calm, it scared me. I hated that I was in here and couldn't be out there with him. I knew he was plotting some shit, and I was scared. We had just begun living our lives, God had spared me, and I didn't want to lose him.

***

Two days had passed, and I was so ready to go home. I hated being in this old ratchet-ass hospital. The nurses were rude as hell, and when you needed them, they took forever. By the time they got to you, you'd forgotten what you needed in the first place. My mama had been on them, though. That lady cussed whoever didn't do their job right, and she got shit taken care of. Any other time, I would have thought that she was embarrassing, but not now. These bloodclaat people needed to be put in their place. . . .

"Bitch, I can't wait until you get out of here, so we can do road," Sophia said as she sat by my bedside.

"Bitch, I can't wait. I swear, the first thing I'ma do is ride that dick."

"Oh my God. You're a fucking fool! Bitch, you almost die, and the first thing you want to do is fuck? You not easy at all," she said and burst out laughing.

"Bitch, just because I got shot don't mean my pussy don't work. Every time that bwoy come up here and get close to me, all I'm thinking about is feeling him up inside of me."

"Keep on and him soon get you pregnant."

"Bitch, his pull-out game is strong. Plus, I take the pill faithfully. I love Gaza, but I'm not ready to be no baby mother. I'm trying to be the wife. Baby mother don't carry no weight no more."

Sophia nodded. "I hear you, me gyal. At least you lucky Gaza don't have a whole heap a baby mother. Oneil have three baby mother and still want to breed me. Gyal, I have the depo shot, but he doesn't know. Every time when my period come, he get angry, talking 'bout he don't know why I can't get pregnant. I don't pay him no mind. I just look on him and don't make him no wiser. Until that nigga put a ring on this finger and move us out of the slum ain't no baby growing up in here."

"Girl, I hear you."

She stood and stretched. "Anyways, I'm about to hit the road. You know they still have curfew in effect, and after what happen to you, I'm scared to be out at nights. Oneil get him a little gun, just in case anything pop off."

"Well, bitch, you goin' to be all right. I pray for me and you every night. God knows I don't know what I would do if anything happens to you."

"Bitch, me is a God bless girl. Trust me, them dutty bwoy them can't touch me. Anyways, babes, I will link you tomorrow yah."

"All right, baby."

After Sophia left, I was tired, so I decided to take a nap. Gaza was in St. Elizabeth, handling some business, and I doubted he would be back in time to visit me. Even though I was missing him, I needed time to catch up on some much-needed rest.

Chapter Ten

Gaza

It was the wee hours of the morning, and Leroy and I was on a mission. Soon as Camille had told me that some niggas approached her and sent threats, I had got on it. Leroy had put the word out that we was offering about fifty stacks for info. I had been trying to get at the niggas, but it had been too late. They had got at Camille first.

That hadn't deterred me. I was even more determined to get these niggas. After making sure Camille was going to be safe, I had got with Leroy and had put a plan in motion. I was well aware that the police had my name and was asking questions about me. I definitely wasn't trying to be on their radar any more than I already was.

I was dressed in all black from head to toe. A few days ago, Leroy had found an old car that was for sale in St. Catherine. We had paid the old man cash and had driven off in it.

"Yuh ready, dawg?" I said as I sat in the passenger seat of that car.

"I was born ready," Leroy said as he pulled off. We knew that the police was out and the curfew was in place. Leroy had this soldier on the payroll, and he had given us the hours of police operations in every area we were driving through tonight. That was perfect for us to get at these niggas.

"Yo, Father, yuh think Gio looking down on us and saying these niggas make me proud?" Leroy asked me as he drove.

"Yo, Leroy, Gio is right here with us, dawg. Sometimes I can smell that grabba that he puts in his weed. Trust me, the dawg is right here with us, yo."

We continued reminiscing about the great times we had had together, even though we had missed out on a great deal when we were in prison. Nonetheless, prison walls hadn't been able to separate us.

"That's the bar right over deh." I pointed to the right.

Leroy made a right turn and parked on the side of the building. The word we had got was that these three niggas frequented this bar every night, and even though there was a curfew, the owner paid off the police so that the bar could stay open when everywhere else had to close.

It was well after 2:00 a.m., and the streets were clear. The soldier nigga was right. The police team had left out right at 2:00 a.m. Leroy cut the car off, and we scooted down in our seats in the dark and just waited for our prey. Ten minutes passed, then twenty minutes. Our informant might be wrong.

"Yo, yuh think we got good information?" I quizzed. I was kind of feeling disappointed.

He tapped me on the leg, then pointed toward the front of the bar. I lifted my head to peek, and I saw a bunch of niggas exiting the bar. Two went to the right, and three went toward Langston Road.

"That's the bwoy them that," Leroy whispered.

"Yuh sure yo?"

"Mi know the tall one. He used to play ball for Ardenne. I know how the bwoy build. Him and one of the bwoy that get shot are cousins. Trust me, it's them."

"All right, then. A this it."

Leroy waited for a few minutes, until the three dudes heading toward Langston Road had cut down the lane, before he started the car. I pulled the chopper off the floor and sat it in my lap. He kept the lights off and drove toward the niggas. I pulled the gun up. . . .

Bap! Bap! Bappp!

All you saw was bullets flying out the window and niggas dropping to the ground like flies. I fired over fifty shots. After I fired my last bullet, Leroy pulled off slowly and waited a few; then he cut the lights back on. And just like that them niggas became casualties of war. They should've thought twice before they sent threats to me and violated my bitch. Now baby girl could feel safe again. . . .

Everything was flowing right with the business. I had made my overseas shipment on time and had got my money. The Big Man was happy that I had come through like I said I would. He had thanked me over and over and had even offered me two of his bitches. As much I would have loved to smash that little Asian one, I had been taught never to mix business with pleasure. So I'd thanked him and left.

Now me and Leroy were on our way to St. Elizabeth to meet with a ganja farmer. Gio had put me onto him, and now that Gio was gone, I was still trying to do business with this farmer.

"Yo, is this bush, Father," Leroy sighed.

"I agree. I have no idea how people live up in places like this. Look at the big old pothole. Don't tell me the people keep voting for these niggas and the place is like this."

"This pure fuckery. If the car go too far to the right, we not going to live to tell it. Boy, Jah know them doing the people them that live in the country bad."

"Yo, we almost there," I said. "This a town call Jointwood. Even though it look like this, it have some of the best ganja in Jamaica. Them man yah a hard workers too, you know."

"This is close to St. James. I heard the scamming thing hot down here too," Leroy noted.

"Is that, me brethren telling me. A pure gun and scamming thing going on down here. Country man with guns. Yo, I remember back in the day, when all country man had was machete. Now all machine gun, the bwoy them have."

"Yo, let's get what we getting and cut. I would hate to pull the chopper out of the trunk," Leroy said. I knew he was dead-ass serious.

"Yo, is that house right up on the hill." I pointed to the house on the left.

Leroy pulled over and stopped in the yard. I jumped out of the car but was stopped in my tracks by a mongrel dog that looked like he was searching for his next meal.

"Yo, what a gwaan, mi brethren?" my nigga Kojak said as he stepped into the yard.

"Yo, what's good, yo?"

Kojak pointed at his house. "Y'all come inside, man. It too hot for I to be in this heat right now."

"Leroy, come on," I called. "This is the brethren that I was telling you about."

Leroy turned off the car and climbed out. He and Kojak exchanged daps, and we walked into his house.

We took a seat at the kitchen table, and Kojak put some weed on the table, some wraps, and a bottle of white rum.

"So the man them cut out Gio?" he said.

I shook my head. "Jah know, star. That one was hot. Now I can't believe say mi brother gone."

"Yo, I was shocked when I got the word, 'cause Gio was a thorough youth," Kojak said. "I been doing business with him for 'bout the past four years or so, and every time he came through. He was nothing but real. I can't believe what the pussy them do to the bredda, star."

I looked him in the eye. "Well, just know it's handle . . ."

"Enough said. Now let's drink and send one up for Gio."

We sat there drinking, smoking, while we reminisced about Gio and the good days.

When everyone at the table grew silent, I said, "So, Kojak, let's discuss business."

"Talk to me."

"You know Gio is gone, but I'm still here. With that said, my operation is bigger and better. I'm moving major weights overseas, and I need to know you can meet the demand."

"Ha-ha. You must ain't seen my field. I can meet any demand that is required."

"Right now I need only 'bout five pounds, but next week I'ma need another two hundred pounds to ship out to Miami."

"Now you talking . . . I got you. Just tell me the date, and I will have everything ready for you."

"Yo, what's your price for the two hundred pounds?" I asked.

"Well, you Gio nigga, so you get the same price he get. So I say a hundred grand."

"Sounds good. Do you dry it and compress it?"

He nodded. "Whatever you want. Just say the word, I get it done."

"A'ight, deal."

"I tell you what. Take this five pounds as a token of appreciation. You deal with me proper, I deal with you proper."

"Bless, Father. I appreciate it."

After he handed the ganja to me, we talked for a little while longer. The thunder started to roll, and the place was getting dark. I was ready to get up out of the place before the rain started falling. The way these roads were set up with the potholes, we would be lucky if our car made it up out of here.

The next morning I woke up early and dialed Leroy, who had managed to drive us back from St. Elizabeth without a hitch, despite the rain and potholes.

"Yo, Leroy, I need you to roll up the niggas. We need to have a meeting. I've put this off way too long. Plus, we can use them to do some shit within the organization. We also need to see about this scamming money. Before Gio died, he told me that some money came up missing. We were supposed to discuss it the day after the operation, but we didn't get a chance."

"Yo, Father, how about if the meeting is at ten dis morning around by my place?" Leroy said.

"A'ight, bet," I said before we hung up.

I got dressed and then headed out. The meeting was at the place that Leroy had down on Hagley Park Road. This was our new spot, because doing business down by the Gully was out of the question.

As I drove, all different scenarios ran through my head. *It better be a good fuckin' reason why that money has come up short*, I thought. I strongly believed in loyalty and would hate for one of the niggas that Gio and I had trusted to be taking from us. I treated these niggas like family. When it came to disloyalty, I knew that death was the only solution.

The block was quiet, as usual. I scoped out my surroundings before I pulled into the back. Everything seemed straight. I checked my waist. Even though those were my family inside, I still came prepared, as money was the root of all evil. I entered without warning. I could hear niggas' voices blasting from the living room. I made my way there, and when I stepped into the room, heads turned and everyone focused on me.

"What's up, fellas?" I said, then gave each of them dap.

"Whaddup, boss?" they chorused.

I took a seat across from Leroy. I didn't waste any time. I had come here to handle business, so I got to it immediately.

"I know we all took a hit when Gio and Ratty passed, 'cause they were family, but we need to get back to business. We got money to make in these streets. With us slacking, other niggas are able to eat out here. Fuck that. If anybody eating good, we goin' to be the ones to eat. The rest of them bwoy can suck them muma."

The entire time I spoke, I kept my eyes glued on this one little nigga. He was the one that Gio had had some kind of altercation with before his death.

I went on. "Yo, before Gio died, he told me some money come up missing. Listen, y'all, I 'on't know who fuck wit' mi bumboclaat money, but bottom line is somebody gon' pay with them pussyclaat life." I paused for a second, then continued. "I can't say fo' sure who the pussyclaat nigga is. But best believe I'ma find out, and when I do, I'ma chop yo' fucking head off."

"Yo, Father, no disrespect still, but Gio was a pussy. When 'im was here, him treat people fucked up, and now him gone, people a glorify him. Gio probably the same nigga that take the money and now trying to put the blame on another man."

I stood there, looking at this little bitch-ass nigga disrespect my brother. My mind was racing. Wasn't sure how I wanted to handle it.

"You finish?" I growled.

"What you mean?" he said.

I pulled my gun and aimed it at him. "See, little nigga, that nigga that you kill was mi brother, mi partner. You took him away from the people that love him, because you jealous. Yo, tell my brother I say, 'What's good?'"

Pop! Pop! Pop!

I fired three shots into that nigga's torso, forcing his lifeless body to collapse on the floor. The remaining three niggas in the room looked at me, then looked at his body.

"Yo, anybody else want to disrespect mi bredda?" I snarled.

They looked at me, then shook their heads no. I wasn't here to play with niggas. Either they was going to show respect or be cut down. . . .

"Yo, Leroy, call in the cleaning people."

"Say no more, Father."

"Now back to business. Meet here tomorrow at eight a.m. sharp. I got a shipment going out in two days. I need to get it straight."

I got up and walked out without waiting for a response, then slammed the door behind me. I was pretty sure these niggas had got the picture that I wasn't playing around with them. I was building a clique, and I needed to know them niggas were loyal. I'd dealt with one snake nigga before, so now I was extra careful.

I knew Leroy was one hundred, but everybody else was suspect. I needed to know that I could trust the people around me. If I had to question their loyalty, then who the fuck could I trust? *No one . . .*

Chapter Eleven

Camille

To say I was happy would be an understatement. I was bursting with joy as I walked out of my hospital room. Even though I was using a crutch, I was happy, nonetheless.

"You ready, bae?" Gaza said.

"Yes. Let's get out of this nasty place," I told him.

I didn't care if the nurse was standing beside me. The three weeks that I had spent in here were stressful, to say the least. I'd heard many stories about how terrible the hospitals in Jamaica were, and sadly, I had got to witness this firsthand.

"Let me run and get the car," Gaza said before he dashed off.

"You is one lucky gyal. That man care about you," the nurse said.

"Is not luck, baby. Is me good."

She shot me a look like she was offended. Before the conversation could continue, we stepped through the lobby doors, and at the same moment, Gaza pulled up in his BMW. I could see the look on the nurse's face. I could tell she was feeling jealous. I looked at her, smiled and walked on my crutch to the car. Gaza opened the car door and helped me to get inside. The nurse stood there staring. I decided to be petty, so I waved to her and smiled before he pulled off.

"How you feeling, babes?"

"Better now that mi going home. I was sick of that damn place," I replied.

"Well, just know your man was missing you."

"Were you seriously? So why I call you the other night and couldn't reach you?" I shot him a look.

"Babes, anytime you ring my phone, I always pick up—unless I'm handling business."

"Hmm. Handling business that late?"

"Yo, baby, my business don't have no set hours. When the phone ring, I'm gone to the money."

I kind of had a feeling that Gaza was lying, but I couldn't prove it, so I dropped the subject. I knew Gaza got irritated fast, and I didn't want to start an argument between us right now. I was a born detective, and if he was fucking around on me, I would find out in due time.

Twenty minutes later, Gaza pulled into the driveway. I was happy to be back home. I headed inside, and the first thing I did was take a shower, to scrub that hospital scent up off me. Once I was dressed, I headed into the kitchen, where Gaza was talking with an older woman.

"Aye, babes. This is Miss Doris," he said when he saw me. "She is my grandmother's good friend and the lady that was helping me take care of the house before you moved in. She will be staying in the guest room for a few weeks so she can take care of the place."

"Take care of the place?" I looked at him suspiciously.

"The doctor them say yuh need fi rest up at least fi another two weeks. Miss Doris will make sure of that. She will handle the cooking, the washing, and everyting else."

Okay. Hello, Miss Doris," I said.

"Hello, dear. Mi so happy yuh doing much better. I make you some chicken-foot soup wit' potato and carrots. Mi madder always sey when yuh sick, chicken-foot soup is the cure."

I smiled. "Thank you so much. I'm not really hungry right now, but I'll eat it later on."

I left the kitchen and went into the bedroom. The truth was, I had turned down the soup not because I wasn't hungry, but because I had just met this woman, and I wasn't going to eat anything she prepared until I knew her a little better. I didn't care how sweet looking she was. Besides, most of the Jamaican people were nasty and didn't know how to cook.

"Yo, what a gwaan? Why you behaving like this?" Gaza said as he stepped into the bedroom and closed the door.

"What you talking about?" I asked, pretended I didn't know.

"I see how you make up yuh face when me introduce Miss Doris to you . . ."

I put my hands on my hips. "How long you know this woman before you bring har up in here, cooking?"

"I met her when I first move out here, so over a year now. But my grandmother and her been friends for years. Camille, you know how mi move. I wouldn't just bring anybody up inna mi place like this if I didn't know them. Yuh need to chill out, yo."

"I'm cool, Gaza. Matter of fact, I'm tired, so I'm gonna take a quick nap."

"Cool. I'll be back in later tonight. Going to go up by the place that Leroy and I open up. Hit my phone if yuh need me."

I didn't say anything. I watched as he opened the bedroom door and walked out. As I lay down on the bed, I couldn't help but wonder what place he was referring to. *Hmm. Who knows?* He'd been making major moves. I guessed I'd find out in due time.

Chapter Twelve

Gaza

We'd been going hard at the grind for the past few months. We'd been shipping keys upon keys of raw, uncut cocaine to the United States. My nigga Royal, whom Gio used to do business with, was the one that went on these runs. At first, I'd been kind of skeptical about him, 'cause he seemed like a hothead, but he had proven himself enough for me to trust him.

Leroy, the Big Man, and Royal had all built an airtight organization that was pulling in millions of dollars weekly. We also had about six street niggas who did the everyday handling of certain parts of the business. I was careful not to fuck around with no strange niggas. Call me paranoid, but every nigga that wanted to do business with me was suspect. I was moving enough coke and bringing in enough money to catch the attention of the police in Jamaica and the United States

Feds. Every other week, I made sure I changed out my throwaway phone, and I never spent more than a few seconds with any nigga on the phone. Last time I got indicted, they had had hours and hours of phone recordings on me and the crew. I was determined never to go back into the belly of the beast, and to ensure this, I had to make sure that I was more than careful and that I trust no one.

Life was definitely good. I had bought Camille and myself a bigger place. It was an eight-bedroom, eight-bathroom mansion up in Cherry Gardens. I had also got her into driving school before I bought her a baby blue Benz. I mean, if I was stunting, then my bitch got to be stunting also.

I wasn't no fool, so I knew I needed to make sure money was stashed away just in case some shit popped off. I had had a safe built in the crib also, and there I kept over a hundred grand, just in case I needed some emergency money.

The bar that Leroy and I had opened was really a cover for most of the business we handled. If you were on the outside looking in, you would see an international sports bar. Bitches walking around in booty shorts, heels, and little tank tops. Not just any kind of bitches, but some of the finest bitches in Jamaica. I even have a bad little Haitian bitch named Trina working up in there. I had done smashed her a few times, but I had to keep it on the low 'cause Camille had started running the bar. I didn't trust these bitches to handle my money, so Camille was the only person who fit that position. She had even brought her homegirl in to work the bar.

It was Sunday and definitely a laid-back day. I hadn't got in from Westmoreland until the wee hours of the morning, and a nigga was beat. Camille made me breakfast: ackee and salt-fish with roasted breadfruit and a fresh glass of papaya juice. One thing I respected about Camille was that even though we had a helper, she didn't allow her to cook all the food. If Camille was at the crib, she was going to wake up in the morning and make sure she fixed her man's plate.

"Hey, babes. I got something for you," I said as she lay with her head on my chest, rubbing it.

"What? Some dick?"

"Well, yuh know yuh can get that anytime."

I reached over in the drawer and pulled out a pink, diamond-plated baby nine and offered it to her.

She looked at it but didn't take it. "What this for? Yuh crazy. I don't play around wit' gun."

"Camille, listen to me, yo . . . I don't know if you don't realize that we ain't living regular anymore. We rich, baby, and wit' that come jealousy and envy. I want you to start paying attention to everything. When you're coming home, make sure you're not followed, and when yuh at the club, keep the back office lock when you're in there. Don't allow nobody to come back there, not even yo' homegirl. Your man is a kingpin, and I run a powerful organization. People gonna try to bring me down, and they will try from every direction. You my woman, and I need to know you gonna help me protect this kingdom."

She looked at me, looked back down at the gun, and took it out of my hand. "I don't know how to use this thing."

"No worries. Later this evening we going driving on the back road, and I will teach you. You have to make sure if you pull it, you're ready to use it."

"All right, baby. If yuh say I need it, then that's what is."

I looked over at Camille. I tried to hide my feelings for her and I might fuck other bitches, but I loved her. When I finished getting this money, I planned to pop the question to her. I was not no fool; I knew this business wouldn't last forever. I needed to get what I was getting and then get out fast. My plan was to get out of this business in a year at the latest. That meant I had a six-month plan to get rich and get out.

After taking Camille out for dinner that evening, I decided to drop by the club. I was in the mood to drink and kick back. Maybe I could catch a game of pool with Leroy. The other day I had beat him and had got seventy-five grand up off him. When I reached the club, I parked in the back, by Leroy's Lexus, and got out. I made sure the coast was clear before I stepped through the entrance.

"Yo, boss, come through," the doorman, Blair, greeted me as we exchanged daps.

I walked through the club, which was crowded. I spotted a few homies sitting at the bar, and I hailed them while I walked through. I saw Leroy sitting at the other end of the bar, so I made my way over to him.

"What's good, Father?" he greeted me, and we embraced.

"Just here cooling. See it's a full house tonight."

"Was just sitting here, thinking the same thing. Royal is on his way up here. He just came back."

"Oh word? Did everything go as planned?"

"Everything copacetic, Father. I say we on our way to being a bunch of rich-ass niggas," Leroy said, obviously under his liquor.

I waved for the bartender. She headed over.

"Hey, boss man. What you drinking on?" Sophia said all seductively. I swear, if she and Camille were not friends, I would smash that ass.

"Let me get a shot of Patrón on the rocks."

"Okay, boss man," she said, putting it on extra.

After she walked off, Leroy tapped my arm. "Mi know you must fuck da catty deh."

"Nigga, yuh trippin'. That's my bitch best friend. I can't even risk it."

"I hear you dawg, but I see how the gyal a pree yuh."

"Man, you a funny nigga." We then burst out laughing.

Just then Sophia came over, a glass in her hand. "Here you go, boss." She placed the small glass on the counter, smiled at me, and walked off. The tights she had on had her ass looking juicy and fat. I'd been trying not to look at her in that light, but since my dick was twitching around in my pants, I couldn't help it.

I waved for her to come back. She walked slowly toward me, like she was playing with me.

"Come over here," I said.

She leaned in toward me at the counter.

I leaned in and whispered in her ear, "Meet me in the office in five minutes."

She didn't respond with words, but her smile was enough to let me know she understood my language. I turned my attention back to Leroy.

"I'ma be in the office for 'bout twenty minutes. If that nigga come, keep him out here."

"All right, Father. What if Camille come?" That nigga burst out laughing.

"You is a really pussy, you know that?"

We both started laughing. I shook my head and walked off, still laughing.

I opened my office door and entered. The only thing on my mind was this pussy I was about to tear up. I quickly rolled me a blunt and took a few pulls before I heard banging on the door.

"It's open," I yelled.

Seconds later, sexy, vibrant Sophia entered the dimly lit office. I was sitting on the sofa.

"Yes, boss man? You wanted to see me," she said as she walked toward me.

I got up, walked over, and closed the door. I then took a seat back on the sofa and pulled my dick out.

"Yo, come suck this," I demanded.

"Oh my, but you . . ."

"Yo, Sophia, stop play yo' bloodclaat game wit' mi'. Is long time yuh want me to fuck yuh, so come give me a headers."

Without hesitation, she dropped to her knees and slowly started beating my dick, bringing it to a full erection. She inserted my monster dick into her mouth, not giving it a chance to get limp. She then started licking it slowly while massaging it up and down. I was horny as hell, and this bitch was playing. I grabbed her head and pushed it down on my dick.

"Yes, bitch, this is what I'm talking about," I said as Sophia moved her head up and down, giving me the best feeling ever.

"Damn yo!" I yelled.

I had tried my best not to yell out, but this bitch was a beast. She was sucking on my dick like she was famished. She continued spitting on my dick while deep throating it. I could tell she was enjoying what she was doing, because of the way she held the dick and kept smiling. My knees were trembling like it was a cold winter night. I held on to the sofa as my veins got bigger.

"Goddamn! Damn it, man," I moaned out as her neck, her mouth, and her tongue were in full throttle as she sucked the life out of me. Within seconds, my juice was gushing out of my dick and into her mouth. Surprisingly, she didn't flinch. Instead, she quickly cleaned my dick off with her tongue.

I jumped off the sofa, pulled her up off the floor, grabbed her by the neck, and threw her on the sofa. Her back was arched as I pulled her tights down, along with her panties, revealing her nicely trimmed pussy. She quickly stepped out of the clothes. I used my right hand and reached between her legs.

"This is what you want, bitch?" My fingers slipped into her wetness. I couldn't front. Her wet, fat pussy was turning me on. I was at the point of no return.

"Me don't care what you call me. Just fuck me right now. Hurry up," she said.

I removed my fingers and tasted it while looking her in the eyes. I loved how it tasted and was tempted to take a lick, but I couldn't risk it. She wasn't my main bitch, eating pussy was taboo in Jamaica, and a nigga with my status couldn't afford to have his name wrapped up in no shit like this.

"I'ma gi yuh this dick, gyal." I opened her legs wide and sank my dick all the way into her pussy.

"Fuck this pussy. Me want yuh bad, Gaza. Fuck the pussy," she whispered in my ear. "Oh shit. Fuck this pussy harder." She spread her legs wider, wanting to feel every inch of my wood.

"All right. Yuh ask fi it," I muttered, thrusting all this dick all up in her, not giving a fuck that she was screaming.

This bitch definitely could fuck. She threw her pussy back, matching my thrusts.

"This is what you ask for," I said. I had both hands around her neck while I penetrated her insides. Within seconds her world came tumbling down when I bust all up in her.

After we were finished, she cleaned herself off and left out without saying a word. I was still feeling weak in the knees. This bitch was a beast in the bed, as crazy as it sounded, and I didn't think I was going to stop fucking her anytime soon. . . .

I used the bathroom in the office and washed off quickly. I couldn't risk going home and having Camille smell sex on me. I exited the office just like nothing had happened. I peeped the homie that I was waiting on sitting at the bar with Leroy. They were drinking and chopping it up.

As I walked up to the bar, Royal caught sight of me from the corner of his eye.

"Gaza, my nigga." Royal turned around to face me. We exchanged daps and a quick hug.

"Good to see you back on this side. How was things?" I inquired.

"Everything cool. Made it on time, money deposited, and they ready for the next shipment."

I noticed a few people getting close to us. "Get you a drink, Royal. Then let's all go in the office and handle business."

Sophia handed Royal a shot of Grey Goose, and then we walked into the office and took a seat. I didn't know what it was, but for some reason, Royal was kind of behaving strangely.

"Yo, you sure everything straight? No police or nothing?" I asked him.

"Son, I told you, everything good. Check yuh account. Money deposited."

"A'ight. Well, let's drink to this and discuss some more business."

"Boss, I got a big proposition for you. This one is so huge that after this, we can retire," Royal announced.

I shot this nigga a look to see what the fuck he was talking about.

He went on. "I met this duo in New York that are looking to make some major buys of the coke—"

"You *met* them? So you telling me, two people just walk up to you and want to buy coke from yuh? What's missing out of the picture?" This shit didn't sound right to me, and I started to feel uneasy.

"Nah, brethren, they used to do business with Knox. Me know you know the big kingpin nigga

Knox. A nigga murder him a few months ago and leave all him client them scrambling to find new supplier. One of my niggas in New York tell me about them. Mi meet up wit' them, trying to get a feel a things. I don't mention yo' name or nothing. Them real legit, yo . . . It's a brother and sister, and them have the tristate on lock with the coke. They have an organization that they deal with, and nobody outside of it. Trust me, I wouldn't bring yuh in no fucked-up situation. At the end of the day, it's up to you still. I'm just telling you this is huge for us. Might have to do a few more runs and done."

I sat there listening attentively. I looked over at Leroy, and I could tell he was deep in his thoughts.

"Yo, I don't know 'bout this. Jah know I don't like how it sound," I said.

Royal inched forward in his chair. "Brethren, I'm telling you, them not the Feds. While I was up there, I went to their crib and everything. Was around a few family members. Trust me, this is the big break we need."

"Yo, I need a few days to think about this. This don't mean I will do business with them. Bring them here. I can smell Feds from a mile away. If they legit, we can do business. If they're not, I'm going to kill them and then you," I said with everything inside my soul.

"Gaza, cool off with the threats and shit. Yuh is my brother, and Gio was my partner. I ain't no rat, and I don't associate with rats. Jah know I kind of feel disrespected."

I shook my head. "Royal, there's no reason to feel disrespected. You is our family, you seet, but when you talking 'bout outside niggas in the equation, we affi be careful. You done know how the Feds set up. Yuh see how them set up Buju Banton. We just have to be careful when we doing business with these American niggas. I know none of us want to see the inside of another prison."

"I get it. Listen, Gaza, it's your call, my nigga. Let me know what yuh decide, so I can make the arrangements. I got to go. Got some pussy waiting at the room for me. I'ma get up wit' all niggas in the a.m."

"A'ight, yo. Be easy," I said.

After he left out, Leroy looked at me. I knew he was waiting to see what I had to say.

"So, Father, what you think?" he said when I remained silent.

"I don't really know . . . I'll have to think long and hard on this one. I'ma check wit' my peoples in New York to see if there was any bust or anything. As good as it sound, I can't jump into nothing big like that without being sure."

"Well, whatever you decide, a dat we a roll wit'."

We sat around talking about the fact that if this was a legit buyer, we would be richer than we were now. It was very tempting, but one false move could bring this organization crashing down. . . .

During the next few weeks, we went on with our daily routine. We made about two more trips to the United States, and everything ran smoothly. I was on edge after what Royal had said, but the more I thought about, the more I inched toward the notion that this was a legit business. I discussed it with everyone in my clique, and we all agreed that we would see what it was all about.

So as I sat in my office one afternoon, I pulled up Royal's number and called him. I figured that he would be getting ready to come back to Jamaica soon.

He picked up on the third ring. "Hello."

"Yo, brethren, how tings?"

"Everything good on my end. Out here by the pool, watching the little one take a swim."

"Oh, okay. Listen, tell the people that I want a meeting ASAP. I will provide the place and time when they get here."

"All right, boss. I'm on it."

I didn't respond. Just hung up the phone. I needed to pay a visit to the Big Man. If I was going to take on that much business, I needed to know that I could meet the demand. I got in my car and headed out.

Luciano's voice echoed through my speakers. "Lord, give me strength to face another day, carry on life's road, carry all my load."

Lately, I had just been in my zone, trying to figure out things. I mean, I was a millionaire now, a Jamaican millionaire, but I was trying to reach US millionaire status. I needed to figure out what my next step would be when this was over. I had battles that I had to fight every day, since being locked up for thirteen years had not been easy on my mental. Some days I would be so angry that I just wanted to wile out, but then I'd remember I got Mom Dukes to worry about. Speaking of her, I was missing her something crazy. I planned on calling her later on tonight. I swear, I loved that woman with everything in me.

Chapter Thirteen

Catherine

My eyes fluttered open, and my surroundings came into focus slowly. Clearly, I was not in my bedroom. When I turned to my left, I saw his wavy hair peeking out from under the covers.

"Oh shit," I whispered before letting out a deep sigh. How in the hell did I end up in bed with him again? After standing up, I gathered my clothes and tried to get dressed quickly without waking him up.

"So, you're trying to sneak out on me . . . again?" Propping his hand under his chin, he stared up at me and shook his head.

"You know we shouldn't be doing this, Miles. You're married and . . ."

"My marriage has nothing to do with what we have between us, Cathy. I told you that I married her only because she was pregnant. Her father is one of the most prominent pastors in the city.

There was no way she could've had a baby out of wedlock, and getting rid of my son was not an option."

Tired of that half-assed story of his, I huffed and slid my feet into my shoes. The sun wasn't up yet, and I wasn't down to spending an entire night with him. To be honest, I hadn't planned on sleeping with him. We'd been having an on-and-off affair for almost six months, and it was time for it to end. The complicated thing was, we also worked together. Both of us were federal agents with the FBI, but Miles had a bit more seniority than me. No, I wasn't sleeping with him to get ahead in my career; I was genuinely attracted to him. Not only was he extremely good-looking, but his intelligence was a turn-on. Then add the fact that he was a little rough around the edges and played the role of tough guy very well.

He had coffee-toned skin, sexy honey-brown eyes, and a tall, athletic build, and he was also ten years my senior. I'd never dealt with a man that much older than me before, and I wondered if I had Daddy issues. My father, Samuel Reed, was also a federal agent, but he had been killed in the line of duty when I was merely ten years old. On the day he died, I vowed to follow in his footsteps. An only child and Daddy's girl, I wanted to make him proud, even in death, by continuing his legacy.

"This can't happen again, Miles. It's over." Looking back at him as I walked over to door, I noticed the smirk on his face. He didn't believe me.

"You've said that before, but here you are." His doubt made me want to try even harder to defy the attraction I felt for him.

Tossing the long tresses of my sew-in over my shoulder, I shot him a look of contempt. "You know you shouldn't have invited me out for drinks, because you claimed you needed to talk. It was all a setup to get me in bed again."

Miles knew that I couldn't drink alcohol without getting horny. I'd tried to have only one drink, but he had kept them coming. I'd also tried my best to keep it professional with Miles, but he was a relentless flirt. I could also tell that if he wanted something, he went after it . . . hard. Gossip around the workplace had confirmed that not only was he a cheater, but he'd also had numerous affairs over the years with female coworkers. I didn't want to believe it, but he flirted with other women at work right in my face. One thing I didn't need was any drama over him with his wife or someone that I worked with. Jeopardizing my career was not in the cards, nor was a continuous sexual relationship with a man I knew I couldn't have.

"A setup?" Miles chuckled and pushed the covers back before sliding his nakedness out of the bed. Damn, his body was breathtaking. His muscular chest and broad shoulders were a testament of his all-vegan diet and fierce workout regimen. Not only was his body a dream, but he was blessed with a huge dick that he knew how to work too. My eyes were on him as he closed the distance between us. "We're both adults here, so don't make it seem like I took advantage of you. You knew what was going to happen when you agreed to come to this room with me."

"You're absolutely right, so don't ever ask me to meet you for drinks again. As a matter of fact, I don't want to see you outside of work, Miles. I'm sure it'll be awkward at first, but I'm okay with us just having a professional relationship only."

"Okay." He shrugged his shoulders before slipping his boxer briefs on. "If you say so. Just know that I'm with it if you want to get dicked down again."

Rolling my eyes, I put my hand on the door-knob. "You're so full of yourself."

"I've heard that before," he said nonchalantly as he stared at me with lust in his eyes. "You could be full of me too if you stop playing games. C'mon, beautiful. You need to take those clothes off, and let's get round two in."

"No, Miles. I'm serious. It's over."

He shrugged and turned to walk into the bathroom. "All right. I guess I'll see you at work tomorrow."

Without saying another word, I walked out of the room and headed to the hotel's exit. It was a good thing I'd driven myself to the hotel. My three-inch heels clicked loudly on the marble floor as I walked out the double doors of the DoubleTree and made my way to my white Chevy Impala. Once I was behind the wheel, tears burned the backs of my eyes. At the age of twenty-seven, I was still single and didn't have any kids. Looking at myself in the rearview mirror, I had to admit that I was an attractive woman.

Standing at five feet seven, I had a curvaceous figure that turned plenty of heads. My Coke-bottle shape wasn't the only thing I had going for me, though. My hazelnut complexion was flawless, except for a splash of freckles across the bridge of my nose. With my slanted copper-colored eyes, long lashes, deep dimples, and full lips, I was often told that I should've pursued modeling. Never wanting to use my looks or femininity to get by, I'd decided to use my brains instead. In a male-dominated field, I was often looked down upon as the pretty girl who wasn't taken seriously. Cutting off any sexual contact with Miles was imperative to keep my reputation intact. Climbing the career ladder was my priority, not climbing on top of a man. But being ambitious made it hard to find true love, and I hoped I wouldn't wake up one day regretting that.

The next morning, I pulled up in my usual parking spot at the FBI headquarters in New York, New York. As I stepped out of my car, the strong wind whipped my hair in my face, making it hard for me to see ahead of me. With a box full of files in one hand, I used the other to move my hair out of my eyes. That was when I saw Miles stepping out of his flashy-ass silver Range Rover. When I said that he was my superior, I meant that salary-wise and all.

"Cathy, good morning," he greeted politely, but I could see him undressing me with his eyes.

"Morning, Miles." Walking right past him, I could feel him staring at me. Not looking back, I used my badge to open the door. Miles was on my heels, and I could hear his feet shuffling behind me. With my eyes trained straight ahead, I headed in the direction of my work area.

There was a new file that I hadn't seen before on my desk, with a memo on top of it explaining that I'd be involved in a new case starting ASAP. It was priority, I assumed, because I hadn't been given a heads-up on starting something new. I'd been swamped with the case I was already working on. Before I could even open the file, Special Agent Morris, who was the head honcho, walked up to me with that usual stern expression on his face. He was an older white man, probably in his fifties, with salt-and-pepper hair and green eyes.

"Agent Reed, I'm taking you off the Montgomery case and putting Agent Simon on that. I want to get you out in the field, so this will be your first undercover operation."

Hearing him say those words had my adrenaline pumping. What I needed was the opportunity to prove myself and what I was capable of. Hopefully, a promotion would be coming too. I'd been stagnant in my position for a while, and it was time for me to move up in the ranks.

He continued, "I need you to pay close attention to the information in the file. This case is top priority, so you must be on your A game. As a matter of fact, if you haven't read the file already, you will have to go to Jamaica for this case."

"Jamaica?" I flipped the file open and took a look. The suspect's name was Donavan, but he was known by the alias Gaza. His rap sheet was pretty long, and he'd just completed a lengthy prison sentence. "But he did his time. Why are we investigating him after he's been deported?"

"We have reason to believe that he's still involved in trafficking drugs across our borders. He's also suspected of other crimes, so we need you to be the eyes and ears to find out exactly how we can infiltrate him and his criminal organization. I don't care what you have to do to get him. Of course, I won't be sending you to Jamaica alone. Agent Paulson will be accompanying you."

My eyes shot up, and he cleared his throat. "Is there a problem, Agent Reed?"

"No, sir, not at all." Miles, of all people, would be going with me? That put a damper on my mood big-time. There I was, trying to leave him alone, and we would be spending time together solving a case on a beautiful, romantic island.

"The authorities in Jamaica are aware of the case, and if for any reason, you need them for backup, utilize them. I mean it. I want you to do whatever you have to do, but follow protocol to a tee, Agent Reed. There could be a promotion on the other side of this for you."

"So, when will we be leaving?"

"We're still waiting for the paperwork to be finalized, but let's say a week or two at the most."

The thought of a promotion in my future made me feel a little bit better, but not much. As the boss man walked away, I thought about how Miles had looked at me this morning. Was he already aware that we'd be working this case together? Had he pulled some strings to make that happen? Part of me wondered why I'd be partnered with him when he was known for having office affairs. Was Special Agent Morris trying to catch me in some shit? Maybe him sending the two of us was a cover-up for him knowing about our affair. But how would he know? I had been sure to keep what was going on between us a secret, and I hoped that he had been too. What if he'd told someone?

Biting down on my bottom lip, I knew that I had to stick by my guns and really stop sleeping with Miles. He wasn't worth me losing what I'd worked so hard for. I'd come too far to let it all fall down for a good piece of dick and a strong pair of arms to hold me occasionally.

My phone vibrated at that moment, letting me know that I had received a text message.

Miles: I'll see your sexy ass in sunny Jamaica.

There was a winking smiley-face emoji at the end of his short message. It taunted me to no end to know that he thought we'd be continuing our sexual trysts while on assignment. What he didn't know was, I was much stronger than he thought, and I was determined to show him just how much.

Chapter Fourteen

Catherine

On the way home from work, I had a lot of shit on my mind. Among my many thoughts was my impending trip to Jamaica with Miles for my first undercover assignment. As excited as I was, I was also disappointed. Of course, they had to assign someone to accompany me, but why the fuck did it have to be Miles? Part of me wanted to ask them to get someone else to go with me, but I didn't want to raise any suspicions. I'd surely be asked why, and I'd have no explanation to give. With a deep sigh of frustration, I tried to stay positive about everything. It would be difficult not to let my intimate feelings for Miles take over, but I was going to defy them with everything in me.

The sound of my phone ringing interrupted my thoughts as I drove. I reached inside my black MK bag for my phone, pulled the phone

out, and saw my mother's number on the screen.
My first instinct was to not answer the call, but
then I decided to see what she wanted.

"Hey, Ma."

"Why do you sound like that?"

"Like what?"

"Like somebody pissed in your iced tea."

"I'm okay. What's up?" I said, wanting her to
get to the point. I was losing my patience.

My relationship with my mother had been
strained for years, and that was for good reason.
Soon after my father's murder, she had moved
on to another man, one named Byron Fields. He
was a very successful defense lawyer who made
lots of money. I often wondered if my mother
had already been having an affair with him
before my father's death, because she married
him less than six months after my dad was
buried. I had hated Byron with a passion since
the day I first laid eyes on him. That wasn't just
because he thought he was going to take my
father's place, but there was something about
him that rubbed me the wrong way. Not too long
after their marriage, his true colors showed with
a vengeance.

"Do you have plans for this weekend?"

"No. Why?" I was surprised she'd asked me
that.

"Well, I'd love for you to come over and join Byron and me for dinner." Her voice betrayed her skepticism, because she knew how I felt about him.

"Mom, why do you constantly try to get me to make amends with that man? You chose to stay with him after what he did, and I chose not to deal with him. I deal with you only because you gave birth to me. Don't make me cut you off too," I spat.

"You'll do anything to make sure I'm just as lonely and miserable as you are," my mother hissed angrily. "You know damn well Byron never tried to do anything to you. You just want me all to yourself, Catherine. You don't want me to have a life. You just want me to continue mourning your father, but it's been seventeen years. It's time to get over it."

"Like you did? It'll never be as easy for me as it was for you. He was my father, not some piece of dick and a check. You're pathetic, *Mother*. I don't want to have anything to do with the man you brought into my life that molested me. He didn't try to. He *did* it, and you can be in denial all you want!"

"Since your father died, you've been manipulative and attention seeking. I got you counseling, but that shit didn't seem to work. There's no proof that Byron did anything to you, Cathy. You're delusional, and you have been for years. I don't know how you even passed the mental evaluation to join the Feds. If you don't start dealing with reality, you're going to be in some psych ward somewhere . . ."

"Please stop!" Shaking my head, I tried not to go off on the woman who had pushed me out of her birth canal. "You know damn well I'm not delusional, nor am I crazy. You've been trying to convince me that I'm loony for years, but clearly, I'm not. That's why I was able to pass my mental evaluation with flying colors. You are the one who's delusional. You don't care about anything but money and your fake-ass reputation. You are a woman who allowed a strange man to touch your daughter. Face it. You are just a money-hungry jezebel who has always used her pussy to get by. Too bad I'm not like you, huh? I'm not miserable and lonely, like you think. I have a life and a career, unlike you. All you have is a rich man and a daughter who only tolerates you because you're all I have left. Don't call me again. If I want to talk to you, I'll call."

"Well, if that's how you want to be, fine! You're selfish, and you always have been. Bye, Cathy."

Pressing the END button, I tried to swallow all the animosity I felt for that woman, but it was hard as hell. When I told her that Byron had slid his hand up my thigh and had fingered me right at the kitchen table after church one Sunday, she scolded me, as if I'd done something wrong. Her exact words were, "Don't you dare accuse him of something like that! You will ruin his career and the life that he gives us. Do you want to be out on the streets?" It wasn't enough that my father had left a hundred-thousand-dollar life insurance policy. She'd blown through that in no time with her excessive spending habit.

I'd just turned twelve when Byron first violated me, and I'd known that Byron was determined to groom me for sex. It had started with lustful glances, suggestive comments, and subtle touches, but it had soon escalated. My mother would be sitting right there at the table, across from him, as he violated me. She'd insisted that we sit beside each other at the table and "bond." We'd bonded, all right.

I often wondered if she had known what he was doing to me and had been okay with it in order to keep him. Before my father's passing, we'd been pretty close, but I'd always been closer to my dad. Oftentimes, I'd felt she was jealous of our relationship. She'd expressed time and time again that I'd taken all her husband's attention. What had she expected a father to do? Ignore his own daughter? I was convinced that my mother needed some mental help, but I had decided a long time ago that there was nothing that could be done to change her state of mind.

Before I could pull up to my condo building, I spotted my best friend, Anya's black Audi parked in my visitor's spot. She hadn't even called me, so I wondered what was going on with her. She'd pop up at my crib every so often, but that was only when she was having problems with her husband. What had he done now? Men were so damn trifling. I hadn't told her anything about my affair with Miles, though. I couldn't, because she was a married woman, and I didn't want her to look down on me for messing with someone else's husband. A married woman seemed to take offense to that type of thing, even if you weren't fucking her husband.

When I got out of my car, Anya stepped out of hers. She swiftly made her way over to me in a semi-jog and fell into my arms.

"Anya, what's wrong?" I asked as her body shook from her sobs.

"He left me . . . for real this time, and he took the kids."

"What?" After pulling away from her, I held her by her shoulders and looked into her teary, pain-filled eyes. "Are you serious?"

"As hell. I got home from work, and he'd packed all his shit up. Then I looked in the twins' room, and their things were gone too. I tried to call him, but he won't answer the phone."

"That's kidnapping, Anya. You have to report him."

"No . . ." She grabbed my arm as her eyes pleaded with mine. "I can't . . . You have to help me. If I get the cops involved, I'll never see Chelsey and Kelsey again."

"Well, what do you want me to do?" I was a federal agent, but if the case wasn't being handled by the Bureau, I had few to no options.

"Help me find out where he is. You have access to all types of shit, being that you're a Fed. Do what you have to do to track him down. He left a fuckin' note, Cathy. It said that the kids are okay and not to look for them. He said if I contact the police, he'll make sure I never see them again. Do you think . . . Do you think he will hurt them?"

Shit. Why was she asking me that? She was the one who had married Trayvon, not me. Didn't she know what he was or wasn't capable of more than I did? "Trayvon loves his girls. He's only trying to hurt you. Don't worry. I'll do whatever I can to make sure you get them back."

Quickly, I led her to my condo, my work laptop in my hand. Once we were inside, we both sat down on the sofa.

As I powered the computer on, I asked, "What's his phone number? I'm going to access the FBI's GPS system. We should be able to trace his location with his phone. I can also access the camera. Let's hope his phone is turned on."

Once the program was up, she recited his number, and I plugged it in. We both crossed our fingers. If he'd turned off his phone, we'd have no way of knowing where he was.

"Do you have any idea where he would go?" I asked her while we waited the results.

"His parents live in Buffalo, but I figure that would be too damn obvious. I don't know where he'd take them, but I'm praying he doesn't do anything crazy. He's been on edge for a while. Ever since he lost his job, he's been acting all erratic, and he's always yelling or breaking something. I don't understand why he's always so damn angry."

It was the cocaine that he used that had become a major problem. She thought I didn't know her husband was an addict, but all the warning signs were there. She'd even told me she found a rolled-up dollar bill with white residue on it on the bathroom counter. Then she hadn't brought it up again, and now she probably thought I'd forgotten. Trayvon was a so-called "refined thug" type, and he had supposedly turned his life around, but I thought he was still shady. He had had a good job as an executive at Coca-Cola but had ended up getting fired. Anya had never told me why.

Anya was a real-estate agent who made a lucrative living on her own and didn't need Trayvon financially, but she loved him. Their four-year-old daughters were her world, and she wanted them to have their father in their lives, even if it was at her expense. I had often advised her to leave him, but she'd always had a rebuttal for why she couldn't. He'd been quick to leave her for the smallest thing, though. Last I heard, he thought she was cheating on him. Anya had sworn up and down that she wasn't messing around on her husband. She had been my best friend since we were six years old, so I believed her.

"Okay, good. We're in," I told her as a moving red dot popped up on the laptop screen. "That's him. He's heading north. Let's go."

My .45 was still in its holster, and I didn't remove it, just in case Trayvon was armed. My laptop was hooked up to my hotspot, so we'd have Wi-Fi while I drove. Trayvon was about an hour away, and I hoped that he'd eventually stop somewhere, so we'd have the opportunity to get the twins from him. Hopefully, at this point, they were safe.

Once we were in the car, Anya held the laptop in her lap. I accessed the camera on Trayvon's phone so we would know what was going on in the car. We could hear everything, but unfortunately, the phone's camera showed us only the car's ceiling.

"Are we going to see Grandma and Grandpa, Daddy?" one of the twins asked.

"No. Now be quiet and eat your chicken nuggets!" Trayvon snapped, causing Anya to flinch as the tears continued to flow down her cheeks.

"They're okay, Anya. That's all that matters. Let's just hope he stops somewhere and gets a room or something. By the time he does, we'll be closer. Okay?"

She nodded and wiped her eyes. "This is crazy. He is convinced that I'm cheating on his ass. I keep telling him that I'm not, but he is in his own delusional world."

After grabbing my bestie's hand, I squeezed it. "I know that he's on drugs, Anya. You don't have to hide anything from me. I know I work for the FBI, but you don't have to worry about that. This is personal. Besides, the Feds wouldn't deal with anything so small and local."

Anya broke down then and shook her head as she spoke. She was crying so hard that I could barely understand anything she was saying.

"He . . . he's on heroin now. He's shooting up and all. I never thought it would come to this, Cat. I really didn't see it coming, and now my babies may be in danger because I'm too weak to be alone." Her head was in her hand as she continued to sob.

"Oh shit. I'm so sorry, Anya. Damn . . ." Not knowing what else to say, I just held her hand as she wept.

"It's not your fault. You told me to leave his ass. I'm so damn stupid. What if he turns his phone off and disappears with my babies? What am I going to do then?"

"If he crosses state lines, we can get the Feds involved, Anya. This is kidnapping, and it's a federal crime if he leaves the state. He won't know that they are involved. I told you, I'm going to make sure you get the twins back."

With a nod, she shook her head and wiped her eyes. All we could hear in Trayvon's car was the sound of some music playing. Other than that, it was silent. Obviously, the twins were afraid to speak, because of their father's temper. That was sad, and I really hoped he wouldn't do anything to hurt them. Trayvon was on edge and unpredictable. He was probably under the influence, and that could possibly hinder his ability to rationalize or even operate a vehicle. What if he nodded off or something while he was in traffic? Every worst-case scenario played in my head, so I could imagine what Anya was thinking.

For good measure, I asked, "Are you sure you don't want me to ask for backup?"

"Yes," she said quickly. "I think the two of us can handle this. I don't want the cops or the Feds involved if we can help it."

She was worried about him getting arrested, and I wanted to tell her not to be more concerned for him than for the twins. I decided not to, though, hoping that the situation wouldn't escalate once we found him.

About three hours had passed when the red dot on my laptop screen finally grew still. We had closed the distance some and now were only about forty-five minutes away from him. Hopefully, he was getting a room or had stopped to rest at the house of somebody he knew. I was sure that the twins were getting antsy, and I hoped he wasn't just making a restroom stop. Once I saw that he'd stayed put for at least thirty minutes, I knew that the chances were high that we would close in on him.

"We're only about thirty minutes away from where he is now," I told Anya.

"God, I hope he doesn't leave before we can get there." Anya rubbed her hands together anxiously, with a nervous look on her face.

"I'm thinking that being that he's been there for over thirty minutes, he's not leaving anytime soon."

"Let's hope not." Anya sighed.

We knew he'd left his phone in the car, because it was extra quiet and the car ceiling was still all that could be seen on my laptop screen. Soon the phone would die if he didn't retrieve it. As soon as that thought came into my mind, though, I saw the scenery change. He was inside a hotel room. The twins were in view, because they were looking at something on the screen. He must've let them play a game to occupy themselves.

"I wish I could talk to them," Anya whispered as she touched the screen.

"You can in a little while," I assured her, hoping that things would go off without a hitch.

Less than a half hour later, we were pulling into the parking lot of a seedy motel in Binghamton, New York. Trayvon was probably on his way to Canada and had stopped because the twins were tired. We'd heard one of them complaining that she was tired of being in the car and wanted to go home. They'd asked about Anya, and he'd told them that she didn't want them anymore. That had really made Anya break down.

"There's his car!" she yelled out when she spotted his money-green Cadillac.

I parked, and before I could get out of the car, Anya was running toward the entrance to the motel's office. We had no idea which room he was in, but he had to be somewhere close to where he'd parked. By the time I made it inside the office, Anya was showing the lady behind the front desk her license.

"Yes, he's my husband. He told me to meet him here, but he must've fallen asleep, because he isn't answering his phone. Can you tell me what room he's in?"

The ghetto-fabulous-looking chick smacked on some gum and clicked on the computer's keys with her long bright red stiletto nails. Her hair and lipstick matched.

"He in room two-twenty-four," she told Anya, without a care in the world, as she grabbed her ringing cell phone.

"Thanks," Anya threw over her shoulder as she headed out of the office. I was right behind her.

She took the stairs, with me at her heels. When we got to the room, I stood to the side of the door, against the wall, so he wouldn't know that I was with Anya. Maybe if he saw just her there, things would be peaceful. If he saw me, he'd have a fit. He had always said that she kept me in their business, and that made him furious. And the fact that I was a Fed and he'd committed a crime would rile him up too. He hadn't crossed state lines, but it was obvious that he planned to. He'd kidnapped his daughters without telling their mother, and that was a crime for local police to handle. All I was there to do was to help Anya find her girls and get them home safely. I had no desire to get Trayvon locked up, but he definitely needed some help for his anger and his drug habit.

"The fuck you doing here?" Trayvon bellowed after he opened the door and saw Anya standing there.

"I'm just here to get my babies."

"Mommy!" the twins yelled out in unison.

"Why'd you tell them I don't want them, huh?" Anya shrieked as she rolled her neck with attitude.

"How the hell would you know that, and how'd you know where I was! You ain't taking them nowhere."

"I know you're high. How I know anything else is not your concern. I won't get the cops involved if you just let me take the twins with me."

Rationalizing with him didn't seem to work, because his response was, "Do what you gotta do, but my daughters ain't goin' no damn where. What the fuck you gon' do about it?"

"Tray, c'mon. You know you can't be a full-time parent to them. You can barely do anything without me. How're you going to afford to take care of them? Huh? Think about what you're doing. If you want to leave me, that's fine, but don't put our girls in a bad situation to get back at me."

"If you don't get the fuck away from me, bitch, I'm gonna slit your fuckin' throat."

The sound of a switchblade opening made me act. With my gun to his forehead, I told him in a calm voice, "Put the knife down, before I blow your brains out. I don't want to do that around the twins, but I will."

"You involved this bitch?" His eyes were on Anya's, and they were full of hate.

"She helped me find you." Anya's voice quivered. "It was either her or the cops."

"She *is* the fuckin' cops!" he spat.

"She didn't want to involve the cops, Trayvon. For some inconceivable reason, she gives a fuck about you," I said calmly. "Now, if you don't want to die tonight, let her take the girls, and you go on with your life. We didn't come here for this, but you took it there. Just do the right thing for the girls."

Trayvon lowered the knife and put it in his pocket. "You ain't gon' call the cops?" He kept his eyes on me.

"No," Anya and I said in unison.

His head bobbed. "A'ight. Put your gun away."

"I don't trust you. Now, get the girls and their things, so we can go," I said firmly, letting him know that I wasn't playing games with his ass.

He nodded and turned around. The twins hadn't noticed the ruckus with the gun. They had been too busy playing their game.

"Girls, you're going with Mommy."

He sounded defeated, and as much as I wanted to get the police involved, I respected my best friend's wishes. "You sure you don't want to turn him in?" I whispered.

"Yes," she confirmed.

Knowing that was a bad idea, I bit my tongue. I wouldn't always be around, and he wasn't going to stop being a problem. Things were only going to get worse, but there was nothing I could do about that.

The girls were handed over to Anya, and I finally put my gun in the holster. Given the look of fury in his menacing light brown eyes as he stood there, I wanted to warn Anya that he would probably strike again. As we headed to the parking lot, she held on to the twins, and I pulled the suitcase that he'd put their things in. Once they were buckled up in the backseat, we hit the road.

"Do you really think this is over?" I asked Anya as I drove.

"No," she admitted. "I'm just glad I got my girls back. If he comes back, I'll be prepared."

"You sure? I have to go to Jamaica for an undercover assignment, and I won't be here to help if he does something. Just promise me that you'll be safe and you'll call the cops if you have to."

"I will," she agreed. The look in her eyes told me that she was just pacifying me.

By the time I dropped Anya and the girls off, it was after one in the morning, and I had to be up for work by five. Still, I'd do anything for Anya and my goddaughters. All I could hope was that Trayvon wouldn't continue to be a problem. I knew better, though.

"You try to get some rest," I told Anya as I gave her a hug in her living room.

"All right. Thank you, Cat. You really came through for me. Not only did you help me get my girls, but you also saved my life. I love you."

"Aw, Anya. I love you too."

When I got home, I stripped and hit the bed. In no time, my alarm was blaring, and it was back to the grind. After an exhilarating shower, I got dressed and headed to work. Before I could even sit down behind my desk, Special Agent Morris walked up to me.

"Good morning, Agent Reed. You and Agent Paulson will be heading to Jamaica on Monday, which is sooner than I thought. The paperwork has been handled. I will email you your flight itinerary before the workday is out. Just make sure you absorb as much as you can about this criminal and his crew, and you'll be ready to take him and his organization down. How'd you like to have your own office, with SPECIAL AGENT REED on the door?" A rare smile was on his face.

"I'd love that, sir."

"Great." He turned on his heels and left me to the hustle and bustle of being a Fed.

When I spotted Miles across the room, smiling in the face of Natasha, this other agent, it didn't even bother me one bit. As a matter of fact, I hoped she'd get his focus off me. Instead, he was eyeing me while he whispered in her ear. Pretending not to see him, I opened Donavan's file and got acquainted with the man that I was going to take down.

Chapter Fifteen

Catherine

It was the day that would start the rest of my life. My adrenaline was pumping as my Uber driver pulled up at John F. Kennedy International Airport. After passing him a tip, I jumped out of the black Altima and grabbed my luggage. I had one carry-on and a huge rolling suitcase. Not knowing how long I'd be in Jamaica, I had opted to overpack. Hopefully, I'd be able to crack the case and get enough dirt on Donavan in a small amount of time. I'd been to Jamaica once before, and I'd loved it, but that had been as a tourist. This time, it would be totally different because I would be indulging in plenty of things that could endanger my life. Jamaican criminals were on a different level of crazy than American criminals.

Before I could get inside the airport, my phone buzzed in the back pocket of my jeans. I reached back to pull it out with my free hand as my carry-on dangled from my shoulder, and I managed to answer the call. It was Special Agent Morris, and I wondered why he was calling me after I'd already been briefed on everything I needed to know. I'd read the entire file on Gaza and his men over and over, to the point where the details were drilled into my head. One of the members of his criminal organization had gotten caught trying to smuggle cocaine into the United States a month ago. He'd had over fifty kilos in his possession. Instead of closing down the drug deal, the Feds had allowed it to continue, and the culprit had returned to Jamaica as if nothing had even happened. The thing was, to avoid taking the rap by himself, he had decided to be a rat and had snitched. Now he was a federal informant and would be working with me and Miles when we got there. We had to keep a close eye on him, just in case he decided to turn the tables and no longer cooperate.

"Agent Reed, who in the hell did you use the FBI's GPS to track, and why? You know that you are not to access any federal computer programs for anything other than federal cases."

Damn. He'd found out about that shit already? "I'm sorry, sir. It was . . . Well . . . it is personal, sir. Although I know that it was against protocol, it was for a good reason, sir." With a sigh, I vaguely filled him in on what had happened between Anya and Trayvon.

Special Agent Morris was livid as he reprimanded me. "You, your friend, or her kids could have been hurt, Reed. You must be aware that the whole situation could have gone left. You had a duty to call the local police and let them handle it."

"I'd do anything for my best friend and goddaughters, sir. It was handled, and the police didn't have to be involved. I know you're pissed at me, and I understand why. I need you to do me a favor, though."

He didn't refuse on the spot, but he didn't say yes, either.

"Uh, I need you to pull some strings to get someone to do surveillance on Anya's house and the girls' preschool, but keep it confidential. I have a feeling Trayvon isn't done with her. The only thing is, whoever you get to do it can't let her know what's going on. She doesn't want the police involved."

Special Agent Morris cleared his throat, and then there was silence, as if he was thinking about it. "Okay," he finally said, relenting. "Send me her address and the address of the school. I have some officers on the NYPD who owe me a few favors. I'll get them on it. I wish I had a best friend like you, Reed, but promise me you won't be so impulsive while you're on assignment in Jamaica. You're one of my best agents, and I'd really love to see you get that promotion. Don't fuck it up."

"I promise I won't," I assured him with conviction.

"Okay, Reed. Have a safe flight, and I'll be in contact soon."

"Yes, sir."

After ending the call, I was relieved to make it in time to grab my ticket and head toward security. That was a breeze with my federal agent badge, and soon I was seated on the aircraft well before takeoff.

"Cathy, come sit with me," I heard a familiar baritone voice say behind me. Of course, it was Miles. Rolling my eyes in annoyance, I looked back at him.

"Nah, I'm good. I have plenty of time to spend with you," I threw over my shoulder before looking straight ahead.

It was a good thing he left me alone after that. After putting my earbuds in my ears, I found the music that was on the memory card I'd inserted in my laptop, and hoped it would hold me throughout the flight. There was a new book on my Kindle that I was dying to read. Now was a better time than any, because once my flight landed, I'd be too preoccupied and anxious to read.

Though it was a little muggy out, the pure, clean air that greeted me once I was off the plane in Jamaica made me take in a deep breath. Damn. The smog and pollution in New York City didn't smell so bad until I had the scent of paradise in my nostrils to compare it to. The feeling of someone gently nudging me in the side got my attention.

"Let's grab the rental car and head to the villa," Miles told me, with an irritated look on his handsome face.

Ignoring his funky attitude, I grabbed my luggage at the baggage claim and followed him without saying a word. Instead of a hotel room, we had been given access to an ocean-side Spanish-style villa to pull off the front that we were members of a crime syndicate. We'd be there under the guise that Miles was my brother from Jamaica. His attempt at a Jamaican accent was so on point that he could fool the natives. I was his American-born half sister. We supposedly had the same father, who had died and left the family drug business to us. Our ruse was that our connect, Knox, had been murdered, and we needed someone else to get the product from. The thing was, Knox was an infamous Jamaican kingpin who had been shot multiple times execution-style a few months ago, and we could get away with that story because he wasn't alive to contest it. The plan was for me to play the part of seductress and get Gaza to trust me enough to do business.

Soon Miles and I had our things inside the rental car, which was a flashy-ass cocaine-white BMW with the pipes on the back. We figured it looked like the type of car that drug dealers would drive, and we had to play the part convincingly.

"You ready for this?" Miles asked as he glanced over at me. He was behind the wheel.

I slid on a pair of dark Ray-Bans. "As ready as I'll ever be." Avoiding his smoldering, sexy eyes, I looked out the window.

"You know, we got a luxurious villa and an ocean view all to ourselves," Miles mused. "There's no telling what kind of trouble we can get into. I keep daydreaming about making love to you right there on the soft white sand by the turquoise water . . ."

"Well, you might as well stop, because it's not going to happen. I'm here for one reason and one reason only, Miles. Besides, I told you that part of our relationship is over, so I don't care if we are forced to share a romantic villa by the ocean. We are here to do a job. Getting a promotion is the best thing that could ever happen to me, and I won't let your horny ass ruin it. Get your mind out of the gutter for once." With my arms across my chest, I huffed in frustration. There was no way I was going to be able to deal with constantly being around Miles if he kept on flirting and trying to get me to fuck him.

"Well, damn, I guess you're serious about that shit. I'm sorry if I can't just stop my feelings for you."

"Oh really? Are those feelings in your heart or your balls? Stop pretending like we had more than a sexual relationship. It was nothing other than that. We are here to get Gaza and his men, not to get naked and fuck. Do you ever think of anything else?"

"Of course I do, but damn, you literally threw yourself at me and now—"

"Threw myself at you?" Letting out a sarcastic laugh, I shook my head in disbelief. "You can't be serious. You literally ate my pussy without my consent on our first date."

"What?" He chuckled. "You wanted it."

We'd got a private table at a restaurant in New Jersey, and after he got me tipsy with a few glasses of wine, he'd dropped down on his knees under the table and eaten me out. That shit had had me fucked all the way up, and after that, I'd been at his mercy. Now I finally had a grip on reality, and the pleasure he'd bestowed upon me didn't have me like that anymore. You could say that at this point, I was over it.

"Well, I don't want it now. Let's just keep our relationship on a professional level only. You might as well get used to playing the part of my big brother." Letting out a sly laugh, I glanced over at Miles.

His jaw was all tight, because he was so arrogant and cocky. He just knew he'd be able to get my thighs to spread for him while we were there, but I had other plans. First of all, I wasn't going to drink anything with alcohol in it. Not only that, but I was determined to keep my distance from him, because, to be honest, Miles was irresistible. As his jaw twitched, he kept his eyes on the road.

"You know what? You're right. We have to focus. This shit could be dangerous, and we have to think with our heads and not our genitals. But since you ain't trying to give me none, don't think I ain't gon' get some pum pum while I'm here."

Shrugging, I told him, "Do what you want to do, Miles. Just keep your head in the game. I'm not trying to get killed out here, and I hope you're not either. We gotta have each other's back, regardless of what happened between us. At the end of the day, we're all we got while we're here."

With a nod, Miles agreed. "Okay, I feel you, Cathy. No matter what, I got your back. That's my word."

"And I have yours too. That's my word."

When we got to the villa, Miles and I unloaded our luggage, and then he headed out to the market to get some groceries and other necessities. While he was gone, I took a time-out to get settled in. The tranquil sound of seagulls and the scenic beauty of the ocean were way to peaceful. As the palm tree fronds swayed in the wind, I stared at the view as if I was in a trance. If only I could live somewhere like this on a regular basis. Don't get me wrong. I loved New York. I was born and raised there, and although I'd traveled to a few places, there was no place like New York City.

A few hours later Miles was back with some much-needed supplies and some authentic

Jamaican takeout. The smell of jerk chicken filled the kitchen, and my mouth watered.

"Thank God you got something that's already cooked. I'm way too tired to cook anything," I told him as we filled paper plates.

"No problem. I figured you could use something hearty to put in your stomach."

We carried our plates into the living room, sat on the sofa, and chatted while we grubbed, and thankfully, Miles kept the conversation tame. In no time, I was full. I returned to the kitchen and put the leftovers in the fridge for later.

"Now, that was delicious. You can't get Jamaican food like that at home," Miles said when he came into the kitchen a few minutes later.

"You got that right."

Miles had finished off his food, and now he rubbed his belly as he stretched. "Well, I'm going to turn in, since it'll be all business tomorrow."

"Okay," I told him with a nod. "I think I'm gonna take a quick shower and then take a dip in the pool."

"That sounds like a plan. I would ask if I can join you, but I'd hate to get kicked in my balls for coming on to you. I promised I'd be tame, so I guess it's best for me to keep my distance." Letting out a good-natured laugh, he threw his empty plate in the garbage and headed up the stairs.

After my shower, I put on a black one-piece bathing suit and headed out to the infinity pool. The scene was something straight from a postcard. As I stared off at the horizon, I couldn't help but admire how simply gorgeous the island was. After swimming a few laps, I felt my body immediately relax. After a few more, I decided to call it a night. When I lifted my wet body out of the pool, I looked up to see Miles standing on the second-floor balcony.

"Mmm, mmm, mmm. You are too damn scrumptious. You sure you don't want to join me in my room? I got a bottle of—"

"Hell no, Miles. Good night." Grabbing a fluffy white towel from the back of one of the lounge chairs, I rolled my eyes at him. Then I dried off and headed inside.

The next day I spent most of my time getting into character. I had to sell the part of a streetwise chick who was heavily involved in the drug game. Although I hadn't been raised in the hood, I wasn't naïve about what went down in the streets. After my father died, I'd got caught up in that world and had a thing for thugs. Once I was reminded of how the gritty streets seemed to love you one minute and then chew you up and spit you out the next, I'd focused on my goals again. After I'd graduated from Columbia with a degree in criminal justice, I applied for the Feds. My test scores got me into Quantico, just like I'd dreamed of since I was a little girl. After breezing right through the training, I emerged at the top of my class of recruits.

For the time that I was in Jamaica, I'd be going by the name Indica, which was a strain of weed. Miles would be going by the name Sway. The premise was that the informant, whose alias was Royal, had met us in New York and had put Gaza and his boys on game that we wanted to meet up with them. It had taken a while for Gaza and his boys to agree to a meeting, because they'd been skeptical at first. However, one thing about ambitious dope boys was they'd often take a chance to expand business. If we could gain Gaza's trust, we'd have enough raw evidence to get him convicted and locked up for life.

We'd all be meeting up at a nightclub in Kingston that was the front for Gaza and his crew's business headquarters. It was after ten o' clock at night, and I was getting dressed for the occasion. The dress code for me was sexy and sensual, since I had to be that boogie, that hood bitch who enticed Gaza and his goons. Gaza was the fish I really wanted to hook, though, but something told me it wasn't going to be easy. I was sure he'd already snatched some ratchet chick who would be ready to ride or die for him. That nigga's mug shots showed that he was fine, so I could imagine what he looked like in person. His one feature that had captured my attention was his eyes. They were cunning and alluring. A man like him was trouble, and that was without a doubt.

The sound of Miles whistling interrupted my thoughts, and I realized that I hadn't seen him all day. Well, honestly, I'd been avoiding him on purpose. Having to spend every waking hour with him was uncomfortable, to say the least. Yeah, I didn't want to have sex with him anymore, but the setting we were in was a recipe for disaster. My physical attraction to him hadn't gone anywhere just because I'd gathered the strength to try to leave him alone. I was only human, so that was easier said than done.

"So, you ready . . . ? Damn!" Miles's eyes widened to the size of silver dollars. "Wow! You ain't never dressed like that for me."

"That's because *I* don't dress like this. Indica does."

"Ohhh . . . yeah . . . Well, if I must say, you are killing that dress and those heels." Shaking his head, he added, "If only I'd met you first."

"Well, you didn't. Why do I have to constantly remind you that nothing's going to happen between us again? Stop with the damned hints, and let's go catch the bad guys. That's what we both became Feds for, right?"

"I didn't say anything was going to happen between us, and I won't force you to do anything you don't want to do. I'm just saying that what we had was more than just some fuck shit. You might not believe me, but I mean it. Now, I know that once we get to the club, we have to pretend to be family, so let me get my eyeful now. No disrespect." Looking me up and down like I was a buffet and he was obese, he had the nerve to lick his lips and shake his head.

"Does your wife know how sorry you are?" I asked him right before I walked off. He followed me.

"First of all, you're the only woman I've ever had an affair with—"

Pretending I was having a laughing fit, I cut that lie right the fuck off before he could finish. "I don't know why you think you gotta lie to me, Miles. I'm not your wife."

"I'm not lying."

"Miles, you're a ho. Straight up. You flirt with every chick you see with a pussy between her legs. I see you all up in every woman's face at work. You even do that shit with those ugly bitches. You don't care, though. Pussy ain't got no face."

Rubbing his chin, he said, "You got that shit right."

When I frowned up at him in disgust, he laughed and shook his head. "I'm kidding. I'm just a friendly person. Just because I talk to women at work doesn't mean I'm trying to get some pussy."

"All right, whatever you say. Let's go . . . We want to make a good first impression with Mr. Gaza."

Chapter Sixteen

Catherine

Gaza's security was on point. Not only did we have to be searched by Gaza's men before we could enter the club, but we also had to be searched a second time by them once were inside.

"There's no way she could hide anything in that tight li'l dress," some chick said, with her top lip turned up. She was clutching Gaza's arm like she was his lady or something. From the way she was eyeing me, I was sure that she was.

Gaza was even finer in person, and I tried my best not to stare. His exotic bedroom eyes, high cheekbones, and thick lips were just a few of his facial features that caught my attention now. His girl was cute, but she seemed to be a little too naïve to fit into his world. It seemed that she was trying, but just like me, she was acting. But the fact was that we were putting on a show for different reasons. She was doing it because she wanted to be with Gaza, and I was doing it because if I wanted to move up in the Bureau, I had to get her man locked up.

"Babe, dis is the peoples mi was tellin' yuh about. Simi?" Gaza gave her a look like he was telling her to stay in line. "Dis is a club, so if di lady wanted to wear a li'l dress, dat's her business. Irie?"

"Mmm-hmm," his girl said. As she rolled her eyes, he pulled her to him and kissed her cheek lovingly. His public display of affection was sweet. Most gangstas didn't show that side in front of the niggas they did dirt with.

"Dis is Sway and . . . Indica, right?" Gaza's eyes met mine for confirmation.

"Yes," I told him with a nod.

"Sway and Indica, dis is my girl, Camille."

"Nice to meet you, Camille." I reached out to shake her hand, but she didn't oblige.

Instead, she asked, "So, is dis yuh mon?"

"Who? Sway?" I burst out laughing. "No, he's my brother."

"Indica's mi little sister," Miles said with his fake but spot-on accent.

"Yeah, Sway is from di island, but Indica was born in di States," Gaza explained.

"Well, mi don't see di family resemblance a'tall." Camille shook her head and clung to Gaza even tighter than before.

"Well, dat's 'cause we don't 'ave di same mother, but we 'ave di same father. Indica's mother is from the States, and my father met her after he left Jamaica years ago. Mi was just a yute at di time," Miles explained.

"Di funny ting is nobody mi associate wit' knows you from di island, Sway. Why's dat?" Gaza asked as he lit a blunt full of fragrant ganja.

"Mi lay low and do most of mi business in New York. Mi jus' moved back to di island about nine months ago. Not long dat, my connect Knox got fucked up and shit . . ."

"Oh, hell yeah. Dat's right. Knox was a real shotta now!" Gaza smiled. "So, let's go in di back and discuss business."

Gaza gently removed Camille's hand from his arm. "Babe, mi gotta handle some business now. Mi will be back." He handed her a knot of money, then motioned to the bar. "Get yuhself sum'tin' to drink on."

Balling the money up in her palm, she glanced over at me, with insecurity written all over her face. Something told me that she didn't trust me or Miles, and she was going to let Gaza know that soon enough. In the meantime, I would have to convince him that I was that bitch Indica who was willing and ready to smuggle drugs into the United States for profit. Hopefully, I would come across as a gritty, money-hungry bitch who would stop at nothing to secure the bag. Yeah, I knew all the street lingo, although I didn't really speak that way, and I knew all about the drug game, even though I wasn't really a hustler. One thing I'd learned in life was, sometimes you had to keep the mask on.

We followed Gaza to the back room, where some of his crew were already seated around a round table. The three of us sat down, and Gaza introduced us. As the meeting proceeded, I looked around at all the faces at the table. It was like some cooperate/hood shit. I had to admit that Gaza was organized as hell. He had two armed security guards standing at the door and one standing right behind him. At the table, he had three of his trusted men with him. One of them eyed me, and I knew that he wasn't loyal to Gaza at all. Avoiding his stare, I kept my eyes on the man of the hour. Gaza seemed to focus only on me when he spoke, so I didn't look away. Making steady eye contact with him, I hoped he'd think he could really trust me. It was ironic that right after I had that thought, he brought up trust.

"See, mi don't really fuck wit' mu'fuckas mi don't know. It's hard for me to trust. Mi 'ave always tried to stay out of bullshit, but oftentimes another person can invite bullshit into your life." Gaza turned away from me and glanced at his men at the table. "I already did thirteen years in the Feds." The patois he had spoken at first was gone. "I ain't tryin'a go back. Now, Royal, are you ready to die if you have brought bullshit into my life?"

Our informant didn't even blink as he said, "Hell yeah, mon. Mi know they ain't on no bull-shit. Part of business is expanding. We can't be scared to make money moves, Gaza. I met Indica in New York, and mi saw how she gets down with mi own two eyes. Then, when I met Sway and saw how this nigga livin' and the moves he makin', shit, mi knew we had to get on wit' them. Yuh know Knox was gettin' to that paper. Dey no tryin'a fuck wit' no small shit either, mon. Fifty keys or more at a time. Tink about it."

Damn, he was persuasive, even to me. If I didn't know any better, I'd believe him myself. His eyes didn't give him away, didn't betray any shame or guilt, and so at that point, I thought Gaza was sold.

"Mi not sure if mi is convinced yet. Dis is our first meeting, so . . . how 'bout yuh give mi some time to consult wit' my men? We'll be in touch." Gaza's eyes were hard as he glanced from me to Miles.

"What? Yuh don't wan' to do business, just say
so. It's plenty of mu'fuckas we can get the shit
from. Don't waste our time, Gaza." Miles stood
up from the table.

Playing the role, I stepped in to defuse the
hostile situation. "Wait, Sway. He's got a point.
He don't know us like that, so you can't blame
him for being careful. You know you're the
same way." Lifting my eyes to look into Gaza's,
I continued, "We move weight, not no little shit.
We spend real money and are willing to pay
full price. Keeping our clientele in the States
depends on this deal going through. We could go
to somebody else and pay less, but we'll get what
we pay for. Now, Sway and I both agree that we
want that raw, uncut shit that's at least ninety
percent pure. We don't cut shit, because we don't
have to, but our reserve is almost empty. That's
how much weight we move. If you really want to
move your shit with zero risk and make millions
of US dollars, fuck with us. If not, just say so
now. We don't have time for you to think about it.
Shit, as far as we know, you're working wit' the
Feds to set us up."

Gaza rubbed his chin thoughtfully as he stared
me down. His eyes sparkled, and his lips curled
up into a devious smile. "*Me* workin' wit' da Fed?
Get di fuck outta here." His boisterous laugh

seemed to echo in the small room. "Millions of US dollars . . . hmmm . . . How about we compromise? Mi won't make you wait too long. Gimme twenty-four hours to give dis shit some thought. One fucked-up move could cost me my freedom for life. You must understand that when it comes to business decisions, mi must be thorough. Jah didn't get me outta dat cage just for me to go right back. Simi?"

I had to agree if we wanted to get him. With a nod, I said, "Okay. Twenty-four hours, it is."

Miles shook his head and then headed toward the door. "Let's go . . . Indica."

The sound of chaos caught my attention as we headed out of the office. Club goers were screaming and running like it was a stampede. Without even having to think about it, I reacted when I saw what was going on. After pulling my baby .380 from between my ample breasts, I aimed and shot the man who was holding Camille at gunpoint. Their backs were turned to us, so he didn't even know what had hit his ass before his body crumpled to the floor and blood pooled beneath him.

Gaza gave me a wide-eyed look. "How did you get that shit in here?"

"Apparently, not the same way he got his in here," I told him, alarmed.

Camille ran into Gaza's arms once she realized that she was safe. "He . . . he came in here lookin' for yuh! He shot da men at di door. Tank yuh fi saving me, baby." She hadn't seen me take the shot.

"Mi didn't. Uh . . . Indica did."

She looked at me, but her eyes weren't filled with gratitude. Instead, I saw some type of resentment. Was she mad at me for saving her life? Either way, I felt that I'd done what I had to do to gain Gaza's trust at that point. Even his armed security hadn't thought or moved fast enough.

"Tank yuh," Camille told me in a soft voice and quickly looked away.

"You're welcome," I offered, knowing that Miss Camille was going to be a problem.

"How did he shoot them niggas without us hearing a gunshot?" Gaza he walked over to the dead body and leaned over. When he took a look at the weapon that the man had, he saw the silencer, which explained everything.

"Mi know who dat nigga is, boss. He run wit' them niggas that killed Gio. Dis must be payback for dem bodies we laid out," Royal explained.

Gaza glanced at me. "Mi don't need time to tink. Yuh saved mi girl's life. Come to di spot tomorrow. We're havin' a huge celebration. Mi'll text yuh the address. It's not far from here. We can discuss the details of our transaction then."

"Okay. Good." I smiled and led Miles out of the establishment. We stepped over the dead bodies at the door.

Once we were in the car, Miles shook his head and said, "Now, that was some crazy shit."

"Right. Obviously, someone in their crew was killed, and they retaliated. It's just weird how it was only one dude who came in shooting."

"Maybe it was a family member of somebody they killed. I'm sure shit's going to get way more real and way more dangerous. He won't be the last mu'fucka to come for them." Miles rubbed my shoulder with his free hand as he drove. "Are you okay?"

"Yeah." I moved away from his touch. "He wasn't the first person I've had to kill."

"I know, but . . . who would expect to kill somebody the first night on the job?"

Letting out a sigh, I had to agree. "Yeah, but it got us in there."

All I could think about was a bunch of crazy-ass shottas with huge AKs outside of Gaza's house while we were there tomorrow. What if we needed backup? Something told me that it was about to get way more dangerous than we'd ever imagined. Still, that didn't deter me.

The rush that I felt when I was in the moment of being Indica, the queenpin, was like nothing I'd ever felt in my life. For once, I felt powerful. The look of respect in Gaza's gorgeous eyes had also made me feel a slight throb between my thighs. Okay, so I was sexually attracted to him. There was no way I'd ever act on it, though. Gaza was a cold-blooded criminal, and the reason I'd become a Fed was to take down thugs like him. A thug like him had taken my father's life. Also, I'd have to kill that bitch Camille, despite the fact that I'd saved her life tonight. Besides, my mission was to get enough dirt on Gaza and his crew to lock them all up for life and throw away the key. My pussy was not going to get me in any more trouble. I had a job to do.

The next day, I avoided Miles the best I could. He was all excited about our impending drug buy, but once that was done, the task still would not be completed. Special Agent Morris had made it clear that one drug sell was not going to be enough. He wanted us to dig into the scam that Gaza was also involved in. Not only that, but we needed to be able to pin some murders on him too. Obviously, the Feds wanted enough to ensure that he never saw the light of day again.

After cooking grilled salmon, asparagus, and corn on the cob for lunch, I fixed my plate and carried it into my bedroom. As I ate, I thought about what was to come. Gaza had texted his address to Miles's burner phone. Before I could finish eating, Miles burst into my room.

"I should've locked the door," I snapped. "Damn. What do you want?"

Miles sat down at the foot of the bed. "That mu'fucka wants you so bad, I can smell it." He shook his head, and his nostrils flared.

"What? Who?" I asked, playing dumb. He was clearly talking about Gaza, because I had noticed the way he looked at me too.

"You know who. He was staring at you like he was a pit bull and you was a fat-ass filet mignon."

Taunting him, I let out a laugh. "Please! He was just grateful that I saved his woman. This is not about what *he* wants to do, Miles. As you can see, I have a lot of willpower. Also, I must admit that Gaza is sexy as hell, but this is not about that. He's a monster, and it's our job to put him right back in that cage. Focus. I'm a grown-ass woman, and the way that man looks at me does not move me at all."

"Okay, if you say so, but I saw how you was looking at him too."

"Are you jealous, Miles? Wow. Really? All I wanted to do was get him to trust us. I'm playing the part, just like you. You're so busy being stuck on the fact that we fucked that you can't get into character. My pussy's not worth fucking up this assignment, no matter how good it is."

He moved closer to me and ran his fingers through my hair. Inching away from him, I felt my breath catch when he clutched my waist.

"You're a strong woman, to a certain extent, Cathy. You're defying me now, because this assignment is getting you off. I know you. You're starving for love, and if you get lost in this and let him get close enough, you may blow the whole case. That has nothing to do with me being jealous. True, I've been inside of you, and I know how good you feel. If you go there with that nigga, and he gets one taste of you, it's over. He's gonna fall in love. When he finds out who you really are, what then? What if you fall for him?"

"What the fuck are you talking about? You're really letting your imagination run wild. There's no way I'd ever blow the case for a nut. I'm not like you. I won't ever risk it all for a temporary moment of pleasure. You're reading too much into that meeting last night. The way he looked at me was not about lust. If anything, I think he felt like I was way more useful than you, his crew, and his security. If I hadn't shot the man who had Camille at gunpoint, she'd be dead, and who knows who else."

"Well, his girl didn't seem to be grateful. She knows her man is looking at you in a different light now, whether you saved her life or not. It's clear she feels threatened by you. Also, those niggas are still trying to figure out how you put that gun between your tits and got it in there when they felt all up in them shits."

"We both know the secret." There was a cushion stitched inside my bra to hide the hardness of the tiny gun when I was searched. There was no way we could go up in there completely unarmed.

"A woman like Indica is every gangsta's dream. It's obvious that Camille isn't about that life, Cathy. He doesn't know who you really are, and I'm afraid he'll fall for the illusion. That's understandable. Just don't fall for the illusion of him."

I shook my head. "I won't. I learned my lesson after falling for the illusion of you. Now, please leave. I'm about to take a shower and get dressed. We have to be at Gaza's in an hour."

***

We pulled up the winding driveway that led to Gaza's mini-mansion in the hills, and I tried to hide my awe. The house was twice the size of our villa and even more extravagant.

"Put your eyes back in your head," Miles spat. He was so annoyed for nothing, and it was starting to get on my nerves.

"I'm thinking it may have been a bad idea for us to be on this case together. You're taking everything way too personally, Miles. Get your head in the game, or I will call Special Agent Morris and—"

"And what?" he said, cutting me off. "You're going to tell him the truth about us and risk your precious promotion? I don't know who the fuck you think you're fooling, but it's not me. You ain't that damn stupid."

Not able to say anything in return, because he was right, I got out of the car and hurried toward the front door. By the time I rang the doorbell, Miles was right behind me. The tension between us could be cut with a knife, but we both tried to play that shit off. The door swung open, and there was Gaza in all his gorgeous-ass glory. That man was too damn sexy, and I started to wonder if I'd be strong enough to do what I had been hired to do. A bitch damn sure hated being human. *Shit!*

"Sway, Indica, mi glad yuh could make it. C'mon in." He gestured with his hand, and we walked over the threshold. As he closed the door, he added, "And you don't have to worry about some shit poppin' off here. This place is top secret."

"Who's worried?" With a smile, I reached for a glass of champagne on the tray that a server was carrying.

"That's Ace of Spades, beautiful. Enjoy." Gaza kissed my hand, and Miles rolled his eyes in annoyance. "Mingle and enjoy yourselves. We'll get down to business soon enough." Gaza walked off, but before he did, his eyes bored into mine.

I took a sip of bubbly, trying to pretend that I didn't feel Miles staring at me.

"See what I mean?" Miles scoffed.

"No," I protested. "That shit is all in your head."

"No it's not." As he looked around, he said, "I don't see his girl. He must not have invited her, so he can be all up on you."

"Oh, my God," I muttered before I walked off. His ass really needed to get a grip. What the fuck was his problem? I'd been given the go-ahead to do what I had to do to gain Gaza's trust. The thing was, it had been only twenty-four hours since we'd first laid eyes on each other. Miles had no reason to read so much into the way that man looked at me. At that point Gaza hadn't crossed one line.

Miles was right behind me. "You have to admit that there's a reason she's not here," he said. "I know how a man like him thinks. He's going to try you, so he can get back to the United States. He thinks he can use you for a come up. That chick he's with can't give him what Indica can."

"I thought you said you was going to get some pum pum while you're here. I think you should, big bro. There's plenty of beautiful women in here." With a fake-ass smile plastered on my face, I wanted to slap the shit out of Miles.

"Right now, I'm more concerned about you giving yours up." He narrowed his eyes at me.

"Not that I really give a shit about what you think about me, but don't act like I'm some slut who'll fuck anything moving. I'm not like you. Now, this time when I walk away, don't follow me. If I need you, I'll call your phone." Rolling my eyes, I sauntered off and headed out the double doors onto the patio. *Shit*. I needed to clear my head.

"There yuh are," I heard Gaza say behind me.

My time alone to think had been invaded, but I didn't mind if it presented an opportunity for him to open up to me in some way. He had just met me, but I could be a little manipulative.

"Yeah. I don't do well with crowds."

There was a bottle of Patrón in his hand. "Mi overstand."

After he closed the patio doors, he closed the distance between us. "I want to personally thank you for what you did last night."

"What happened to the patois?" With a smile, I took the glass that he'd just poured a shot of liquor into.

"You're an American woman, and I think I spent enough time over there to speak to you like you're used to."

"My pops was Jamaican, and so is a lot of my family. I understand you just fine."

He nodded. "Your pops *was* . . . ?"

"He died a few years ago. Pancreatic cancer. He used to drink a lot." We hadn't gone over that part of the story, so I had to come up with something.

"Wow. That's tough." He poured himself a drink and sat down at the patio table.

"Yeah, but at least I have Sway." I sat down across from him.

"You don't have any more brothers or sisters?" He put the glass up to his luscious lips and took a long gulp.

"No. It's just the two of us."

"Cool. No wonder you're so close."

Taking a drink myself, I realized it was hard not to say that it was quite the contrary between me and the man that he knew as Sway.

"The way you reacted last night tells me a lot about you. I mean, I gotta admit that I had my doubts at first." His eyes met mine, and he held my eyes in his gaze. "Now I feel like I owe you."

"Well, you don't, but your girl didn't seem to be that . . . thankful."

"Well, Camille's a different breed, I must admit. She doesn't trust you and your brother. She told me that I shouldn't do business with you, although you saved her life and possibly even mine. I mean, there was two of my niggas at the door, but he must've done a sneak attack on them. They couldn't get their straps out in time. It's fucked up, but that's how it is sometimes."

"Yeah, it's the lifestyle we signed up for, I guess."

With a nod, Gaza pulled a rolled blunt from behind his ear and lit it. "You smoke?" he asked.

"I indulge sometimes, but at this point I'm tryin'a quit. I 'on't want a fuzzy head. I'm already drinking."

"I feel you, but this shit here clears the mind." He held the blunt toward me for me to take it.

Weed always made me feel vulnerable, and I'd laugh out of control when I smoked, and the one thing I didn't want was to be under the influence and somehow blow my cover. I didn't even need that damn drink he'd given me. But as much as I wanted to refuse the blunt, I knew I couldn't. After taking the blunt, I took a light puff and blew the smoke out without inhaling.

"You didn't even hit that shit good," he remarked.

After taking a longer hit, I held the smoke in my lungs before blowing it out. Immediately, I was high as hell, and I passed the blunt back. "That's enough for me."

"Wow, you didn't even cough. Let me find out that although you're all woman and you're sexy as hell, you're a real boss."

"Well, a boss can be male or female," I reminded him.

"True, but a female boss is different than a male boss. I need a cutthroat chick like you on my team. Was you planning on returning to New York after we do the exchange?"

"Well, actually, I was."

"Why don't you rethink that and stay here? Do a little business with me. You're very smart and business savvy. What I have in mind doesn't have anything to do with drugs, though. This is about straight cash."

"Talk to me."

In no time he'd given me all the details about the scam that his crew was running on unsuspecting citizens of the United States and other countries.

"Damn. I'm wit' it. All profit. How could I say no?" I said.

"Good. That's what I like to hear."

He passed me the blunt again, and that time, I didn't hesitate to take a long pull. One thing I'd learned about going undercover was you had to do what you had to do to convince a criminal that you were a criminal too.

"So, when are we goin' to discuss the business we talked about last night? It's getting late," I said.

"Where do you have to be? You got a man over here or something?"

"No, I don't have a man anywhere."

"Mmm. Well, too bad for the men here and in the States."

"So, where's your girl?" I asked.

"She'll be here later. She decided to chill with one of her friends for a bit. Honestly, I thought that was best while we handle what we need to handle."

"So, you don't involve her in your business dealings?"

He shook his head. "Nah. She's not that type of woman."

"If she was, would you involve her? I mean, isn't it true that if you love your lady, you'd protect her from risky shit?"

"I guess, in a way." He took the blunt from my outstretched hand. "The thought of my woman knowin' just as much about the game as I do, or more than me, is a little bit intriguin' too."

"You can't have both."

"Truth."

I downed the rest of my drink, stood up, and tried to keep my balance in my high heels as I headed over to the patio doors. The hip-hugging shorts that I wore accentuated my hips and slim waist. I could feel Gaza's eyes burning a hole in my skin as I nodded at him, opened the patio doors, and stepped inside.

About an hour later, Gaza took me and Sway aside and invited us to talk in his personal office. This time, it was only the three of us.

"It's going to take a couple days to get all one hundred of the keys you want. I'm hoping you'll be patient," he said after we had sat down across from him at his desk.

"So, yuh don't have a hundred keys already in place?" Miles quizzed.

"We have eighty that we can get our hands on now, and the rest is in a stash house a few hundred miles away. Like I said, give us a couple days."

"That's no problem, Gaza," I said, with my eye on Miles. Why the fuck was he making that shit an issue? Time wasn't of the essence, being that we had all the time in the world to do what we had to do.

"Okay, great. I'll be in touch." With that said, Gaza got up and walked out of his office, and we followed. He closed the double doors behind us. "Enjoy yourselves. The business part of this is over for now. Have fun."

"No, we're going to head on out. We have some other business to handle," Miles threw in. His accent had almost disappeared.

"I think we can stay just a little longer, Sway," I asserted, hoping he'd get the point that we needed to dig a little bit deeper and watch Gaza's moves closely. The more time we spent keeping an eye on Gaza and his crew, the better. Why was Miles in such a damn rush?

"We have to go, Indica. Now."

As I gave Miles the eye, I told Gaza, "Well, we have to go. I guess we'll be waitin' to hear from you."

"Okay." With a nod, Gaza walked off to continue partying.

As I followed Miles out the door, I was fuming, because our time in Jamaica was all about gathering proof of Gaza's crimes. What the fuck else did we have to do? When we were in the car, I tore into his ass.

"What the fuck, Miles! Gaza literally invited me to be a part of the scam that was mentioned in the file. I wanted to ask him more about it."

"Please! You want to do way more than that, Cathy. I have to protect you from yourself. If you don't get some control over yourself, I'm going to tell Morris to pull you off the case. To be honest with you, he wasn't even going to put you on it. I insisted that he did."

"What? Are you fuckin' kidding me? So I'm on this fuckin' case because of you, and being that I won't give in and fuck you, you want to try to find a reason to get me off the case? You're a real jerk, Miles. I can't believe you! I'm simply doing my job. You don't have one reason to feel that I don't have this shit under control. What you're thinking is personal, and the reason you recommended me for this case was personal too. Well, that's too bad, because I'm going to take this opportunity. I'm going to do exactly what you doubt I can do, and be the one who cracks this case. You need to get the fuck out of your feelings, because this shit isn't about you or me.

It's about getting some scumbags off the streets and putting them in prison, so they can no longer destroy our country with drugs and mass murder. You seem to be more concerned about what I'm going to do with the pussy I choose not to give to you anymore."

Miles didn't say anything. He turned the music up, and some reggae pumped from the speakers, causing me to wish I could go back to Gaza's party to unwind. The weed and drink he'd given me made me want to get loose, instead of being stuck with Miles's uptight ass. He sped down the narrow street fast as hell, but there was no need to worry about the cops, because he was driving like the natives did.

By the time we got back to the villa, I wasn't in the mood to talk to Miles at all. I decided to call Anya and check up on her. Getting lost in the part of Indica made it easy to forget about the fucked-up reality of my real life, but I had to make sure my bestie and the girls were okay.

"What's up, Cat? How's Jamaica?" Anya said when she picked up.

"Work, work, and more work. I can't even enjoy it. How're you?"

"I'm good, boo. How about I finally sold that damned expensive-ass condo in Greenwich Village! That commission check is going to be sweet. I'm thinking about taking the girls to Disney World."

"That sounds fun," I told her.

"Yeah, but I think I'll wait until you get back. I want you to go with us."

"Okay. Hopefully, I'll be getting a promotion soon and will have some extra time off." Not wanting to bring up Trayvon, I did, anyway. "So, have you heard anything from Tray?"

"No, and hopefully, he'll stay away. I contacted my lawyer, and I'm going to file for divorce. We're going to meet tomorrow to go over the details. I got my locks changed a few days ago. The girls are asking a lot of questions, but I'm trying to stay strong about it for them, you know."

"Yeah, I know, and you are strong. You got this."

She let out a sigh. "I hope so, because if not, getting him locked up was a bad decision, and if something happens to my babies, I won't forgive myself."

"Don't think like that. Just be careful and you'll be fine."

"Okay, girl. I gotta go. The girls want me to help them make slime."

"Okay. Tell my babies I said hey and I'll see them soon."

"Auntie Cat said hey, girls, and she will see you soon."

"Hey, Auntie Cat," they yelled out in the background.

A few minutes later Anya and I ended the call. That was a bittersweet conversation, and I couldn't help but worry, despite the precautions I'd put in place. If something happened to Anya or the twins, I'd never forgive myself.

Chapter Seventeen

Gaza

I sat on the patio, waiting for a very important call. This business that I was about to venture into weighed heavily on my mind. I'd done many deals, and I'd done business with niggas from all over the world, but it had always been me that made the move. I had never had anybody seek me out like this, so this kind of had me on edge.

My phone started ringing. I wasted no time in grabbing it off the table.

"Yo, talk to me, brethren."

"Boss, the package just arrived."

"Okay, good. Pay close attention and make sure you see where it will be delivered."

"All right, boss man."

"Killa, this one is a big deal, so mi need yuh fi pay attention, and don't let the package out yuh sight."

"Say no more, boss man."

After I hung the phone up, I let out a long sigh of release. I had my men sitting at the Norman Manley International Airport, waiting for these Americans to come in. Unbeknownst to them, from the minute they landed, they would be trailed. I couldn't be too careful.

I dialed Leroy's number.

"Yo, boss man, wha yuh deh pon?" he said.

"The people are here. The meeting is on fi tomorrow night. Mi need all the security and some niggas in the cut, just in case this shit is bogus."

"Say no more. I'm on it."

I felt relieved, knowing that I would have my street soldiers in place just in case some shit popped off. . . .

"Babes, yuh good?" Camille quizzed as she entered the office, where I was sitting down, watching the closed-circuit monitors that showed the building's entrance and exit.

"Yeah, babes, I'm good," I lied to her.

I couldn't include her in what I was doing. Camille was from the Gully, but she wasn't no gangsta. Plus, in order for me to protect her, it was best that she knew less.

"All right."

She turned and walked back out the door. I kept my eyes glued to the monitor that showed the entrance to the building. Killa had informed me that the two Americans would be pulling up in a late-model black BMW. The cameras were so high tech that they afforded me a crystal-clear street view. That way I would be able to see if there was any suspicious activity from these two.

The scheduled time for the meeting was approaching. I grabbed my gun out of my waist and checked it. I had to make sure I was on point, just in case some shit popped off. If they were on any sort of bullshit, it was definitely going to go down.

I turned my attention back to the monitor of the entrance. I looked closely as a black car pulled up. I looked closer and saw it was the black BMW that Killa had described.

I got up, tucked my gun back into my waist, and made my way out the door. I motioned to Leroy, so he would know it was about to go down. I peeped Royal sitting at the bar, talking to one of the girls. I shot him a text to let him know it was showtime.

I took a seat at the bar, where I could see everything that was taking place. I buried my head in my phone like I was busy, but all along I was watching everything from the corners of my eyes. I watched as a sexy bitch entered, with a nigga right behind her. Her tight outfit hugged her small frame, revealing her assets.

Stay on track, Gaza, said a voice that popped in my head.

Camille met them at the door, and there was an exchange of words. Camille headed toward me, with these strangers close on her heels. I didn't know what had been said, but Camille didn't look to pleased. After I got up and introduce myself to them, I introduced Camille as my woman to kind of ease the tension in the air. Camille was feeling some type of way, so I had to let her know it was cool. I then let her know I was about to handle business.

Royal walked away from his company and headed over to us. Then Royal, the two Americans, Leroy, and two of my trusted top shotta niggas all followed me as I made my way to the office. I entered the room, not knowing what the fuck was going to take place.

I motioned to Leroy to pat the Americans down. I had to make sure they were not wearing a wire. In case we missed something, I had had the office set up to block all transmissions.

"Gaza, this is Indica and har brother, Sway. They're the clients that are looking to do business wit' us," Royal said after we had all sat down.

I nodded. "Yeah, we met briefly."

There was something about the woman, Indica. She was sexy, of course, but she was serious, barely smiled. I sat there analyzing everybody that was present at the table. I ain't no Christian, but I remembered that Jesus sat at the table with the same nigga that betrayed him. I didn't waste any time letting it be known that I had no intention of going back to prison. Royal jumped in immediately, cosigning for the people. There was no way I was just going to go off what another nigga was saying. I told them I needed twenty-four hours to make a decision. This would give me time to get their pics to my people to see if they had ever run across them before.

Later that night, after I had made it home, me and Camille had an argument.

"Yo, where the gun that I gave you?" I asked with an attitude.

I was pissed the fuck off that security had let a motherfucker get past them and that Camille had been put in harm's way again.

"The gun in the room."

"What the fuck did I tell you, yo! You need fi carry that motherfucker every fucking where you go. Which part of 'I'm trying to keep yuh alive' you don't get, B?" I yelled.

"Yuh need fi lower your fucking voice. Mi not yo' pickney, so if yuh ago talk to me, you need to talk to me with sense."

"Camille, come here, mon. I'm sorry, but I'm pissed about the shit tonight. I didn't even see that shit coming, and to make matters worse, that chick was the one that saved you. I'm your man. It should have been me."

I hugged her tight, grateful that I had got another chance with her. God knows it could've turned out differently tonight.

I was up bright and early. This was the day that I had told the Yankee them that I would give them an answer. I hit my nigga up in New York, the one that was supposed to be doing some deep research on these two.

I sat waiting for my nigga Bigga Ford to pick up his phone. I knew him from way back when I used to hang in Mount Vernon. He'd been trapping back then, but when shit got sticky, he'd taken that trap money and put it into a security business. He got clients all over the world because he was so good at what he did. I was hoping that if there was a red flag, he would be able to put me on to it.

"Gaza, my nigga, what's good, fam?" he said when he finally picked up.

"I can't call it. I was hoping that you'll hit me with something good."

"I got the file right here. Hold on a sec."

While I waited, I braced myself for whatever it was that he was going to tell me.

After a minute or so, he said, "I done ran their names through more than one system. I even talk to a friend of mine that's in the Bureau, and he don't think they are associated with any kind of law enforcement."

"Hmm. Okay. So you think it's safe to go ahead and do business with them?"

"It's all up to you. If your gut's telling you shit ain't right, then you might want to run with it, but as far as I can tell, they're good to go, if you want. Trust me, I got their pictures saved on my computer. If anything comes up, I will be contacting you."

"Thank you, mon. I appreciate it," I said.

"No worries. Just have two of those sexy island gyal ready for me when I visit the island in a few months."

"I got you, fam. Be easy."

Okay, so I trusted my nigga's word. This was a green light for them, but just to be careful, I wouldn't be doing the actual drop-off. I'd have my runners meet up with them when it was time to do the exchange.

I was sitting on the verandah, reading the morning newspaper and smoking a blunt, when Camille walked out there. I knew she should be feeling better after I sucked on that pussy real good last night. I was wrong for the way I had yelled at her when we got home, so I'd had to do something quick to make the situation better.

"Good morning, boo. How long yuh get up?" she asked.

"Yuh know mi is an early riser."

"Gaza, I wake up wit' something on my mind."

"Yeah? What's that?" I turned my full attention to her.

"Do you know that gyal and that bwoy from last night?"

"Royal introduce me to them. They looking to do some business wit' me."

"So you don't know them? I don't 'ave a good feeling 'bout them, Gaza."

"Why you say that?" I inquired.

"When I meet people and my spirit don't tek them, something is not right. Also, I see how the gyal looking at you."

"C'mon, Camille. Is this what it's about? Jealousy? Yo, it's a strictly business ting. Nothing else not jumping off."

"Hmm. Gaza, don't mek new pussy cloud yo' judgment. Me telling you, it's something about them. Them claim them brother and sister, but not even an ounce of resemblance. I also see the dirty look that the bwoy give yuh when you and the gyal was talking. It's not a good look."

"Camille, baby, I been doing this for a long time. Trust me when I say I am more than careful. Nothing is not going to pop off, and if it did, trust me, your man gonna handle it. Now, can I get some breakfast please?"

"Of course, Gaza. Me don't want to lose you."

"Me not going anywhere. We good. What I tell you is if I get a couple of these runs, that's it. I'm done. We can open up a few businesses and live comfortable for the rest of our lives. Think about bringing some youth into the world."

"I hear you."

She walked off. I could tell she was still feeling some way about last night. Shit. I understand her concern, but seriously, if it wasn't for the B, Camille probably would be lying on ice in the morgue right now.

After breakfast, I took a quick shower and left out. I had a few errands to run before I headed to the Big Man's house to make sure everything would be straight for the business.

Chapter Eighteen

Camille

I'd seen how Gaza looked at that bitch last night. He'd thought I wasn't paying attention, but I hadn't missed a beat. . . . I wasn't the smartest person walking around, but something was not right. Then it had just so happened that I got grabbed up by a nigga that had made his way into the club, and that bitch had been the only one that saved me. Hmm, if you asked me, it had all been set up so she could gain Gaza's trust.

Earlier, I'd tried talking to him about the feelings I was having, but he'd hurriedly dismissed me, like I didn't know what I was talking about. I just hoped for his sake, our sake, that this bitch and her so-called brother were really who they said they were. Tears welled up in my eyes as thoughts of losing Gaza hit me head-on. I quickly shook the feeling away and went inside to clean up the house.

I was mopping the floor when I heard my phone ringing. I rushed to the front of the house and picked it up. It was Sophia. *Oh shit.* I had forgotten to call her. Last night, when we left the club, I had told her we could hang out today, possibly go get a manicure and pedicure.

"Hello," I said.

"Bitch, you just waking up?"

"No. I'm here cleaning up the place."

"So we not going to get nails done?" she said.

"Yes. Me going to jump in the shower right now. Meet me out at Half Way Tree, because you done know me not coming to the Gully."

"All right. Me already dress, so just call me after you bathe."

I rushed into my closet and pulled out American Eagle shorts and a tank top. Jamaica was too damn hot to really wear clothes. Gaza didn't like when I wear the pum pum shorts them, so I had kind of started dressing differently.

I took my shower, and in no time, I was dressed and out the door. I was excited to be spending the day with my linky. We'd been working real hard at the club at night, so we really hadn't had that much time to get together.

I hate this traffic, I thought as I made my way to Half Way Tree. I had no idea how some of these people had got their driver's license, because they couldn't drive. I finally pulled up over by York Plaza and searched for a parking space. I circled around about three times before I saw a woman pulling out of a space. I quickly pulled into the space right after she pulled out, and parked. I spotted Sophia standing by the water fountain. I got out and waved so she would see me. She did and started walking toward me.

"Yo, my girl, me did not even see when you pull up," she announced when she reached me.

"So you mean fi tell me, as pretty as my baby is, you didn't see her?" I said, pointing to my baby blue Benz.

"You gwaan show off." She burst out laughing.

"C'mon. The nail shop upstairs."

"Yo, me glad you're all right after what happen last night. The Yankee gyal save you still."

"Me not even want to talk about it. Is this morning, me mother telling me she want me to leave Gaza. Before him come in me life, I was good. Now I got shot once and almost get shot last night again."

"Boy, me gyal, me feel the same way like you mother, but I know you love him. Plus, you living good. Look at what you driving, and look at the money in the bank. I'm not sure if I would walk away from all that."

"True. I love Gaza bad, but him lifestyle too dangerous. Him keep telling me just a few more deal and he's leaving the game fo' good."

Sophia shook her head and frowned. "And you believe him. I overhear him and Leroy talking, and the amount a money them have them hand on, I doubt they gonna stop anytime soon. Baby, is you alone can decide if you want to leave him. Let me ask you a question. You think Gaza ever cheat on you before?"

I stopped dead in my tracks and turned to face her. "What make you ask me that?"

"My girl, you know how these bwoy yah stay. I see how him look at the gyal the other night. So you is my friend, and so me just wondering if you think him would cheat."

"Well, me don't trust no man, and in my book all man cheat, but me don't have no reason not to trust Gaza. I mean, if him fucking another gyal, me don't know nothing about it. I love my man, and even though right now we not on no good terms, me nah go run and left him for no next gyal to get him."

"My girl, me hear you. Just keep you eye open, because none of them bwoy can't be trusted."

"So Oneil ever cheated on you before?" I asked her as we walked up the stairs to the nail shop.

"Wha, the amount gyal Oneil fuck, me can't even keep up. Oneil a old dawg, mi gyal," she revealed.

"And you still deh wid him?"

"Gyal, me wit' Oneil only because him have a few dollars. Him not rich, but him is a hustler. Me never go without yet since me and him get together."

I nodded. "I hear you. Anyways, come on. Let's spend some of Gaza's money and get dolled up."

We ended the very intense conversation and walked into the crowded nail salon. While we sat there waiting our turn, the question that Sophia had asked me about Gaza cheating on me lingered in my mind. I'd accused him before of cheating, but it wasn't something that really bothered me. I mean, ain't no bitch ever stepped to me and said anything about him fooling around with her, and when he was home, the phone rang only for business. I swear, I really hoped this bwoy wasn't out there slanging dick all over this place.

"Ma'am, are you ready?" the nail technician asked me, interrupting my thoughts.

"Yes, I am."

I got up and walked over to her station. I dismissed those thoughts before they ruined my day or my already rocky relationship.

Gaza had said that in a few weeks we would be trying to get visas to fly out of this place. I was not going to lie, I was happy he was finally going to give up this life. . . .

Chapter Nineteen

Catherine

I took a quick shower, dried off, and wrapped a towel around myself. I went in my bedroom and sat on the bed, intending to check my phone quickly before I locked the bedroom door. But as I was about to pick up my phone, the door burst open and Miles walked in. Not able to read the look on his face, I let him know about my exasperation with him.

"What did I tell you about busting up in my room? God, can you knock?"

"Don't act like I haven't seen you naked before."

"It's not about that. You are still invading my privacy. Damn!"

"Okay, fuck that. I'm in love with you, Catherine, and I set this all up to show you that. I wanted to let you know how I really feel, and to help you get to the next level in your career."

Letting out a frustrated sigh, I turned to look at him. "I didn't need you to do that. I told you from the beginning that I didn't want you to interfere with me getting a promotion. As far as you being in love with me, that's bullshit. You wanted to do this assignment with me only because you thought we'd have all the time in the world to fuck while we're here. Sorry, but you were wrong. I refuse to be your mistress, but I will milk this for all it's worth and will get that promotion, with or without you."

"Okay, fine. I'm tired of sweating your ass!" Miles shook his head and walked toward the door.

I was ready for him to leave so I could lock the door behind him. "Good. Hopefully, it's over now, and we can do what we really came to do and take down some bad guys."

He turned and walked back over to where I was sitting on the bed. After grabbing the back of my head, he pressed his lips into mine, and his tongue touched mine. I pushed him away, and then I slapped the shit out of his ass before wiping my mouth.

"What the fuck? Why would you do that?" I snapped.

"Stop acting like you don't love me too, Cathy. I know you do. I can feel it every time we touch.

Whenever we kiss." The intense expression in his eyes told me that he was really serious.

"I'm not acting like shit. I don't love you. What we had was just sexual, Miles. What is wrong with you? You're really acting crazy! Get the fuck out of my room before I use my gun again."

"You wouldn't dare." He smirked at me.

"Try me, motherfucker!"

"And how will you explain that to Morris?"

"I'll come up with something."

Miles shook his head in defeat. "Just let me eat your pussy, baby. I just wanna taste you."

"No! Get the fuck out!"

He grabbed my ankles and pulled me down to the edge of the bed. As he did so, my towel unraveled, exposing my breasts and stomach. In a split second, his hands were on my flesh, exploring, but I wasn't feeling that shit. I didn't want him to touch me at all, let alone put his mouth on me. Then I felt his warm, wet lips making a trail down to my belly button.

"Just let go, baby. It's not like I'm a stranger . . . ," he coaxed.

"You're acting like it, Miles. Please, no . . . Stop please!"

"No. That pussy's all fresh and clean too. Just let me make you feel good, baby."

"No! Get the fuck off me!" I pushed his head away, but I wasn't able to move my legs, because of the weight of his body on me.

Before I knew it, Miles tossed my towel to the side, and my naked body was fully exposed. He stared down at me as if he'd laid eyes on the most divine creature. That shit made me nervous, and as I took in the sick, ravenous look in his eyes, I was actually afraid that he would rape me. Still trying to get him off me, I swung my fist and connected with his forehead before he could take my clit into his mouth. That shit didn't stop him. His warm tongue clasped my clit, which was hard against my will. Not enjoying that shit, despite my body's reaction, I was finally able to move my legs and lifted one up, and I swiftly kicked him in his face.

Miles staggered back, clenching his jaw, as he looked down at me in disbelief. "Why the fuck would you kick me in my face?"

"Why the fuck would you try to eat me when I told your ass not to! Get the fuck out now, Miles. I promise I'll shoot your ass!" I grabbed the .380 from my nightstand and pointed it in his face.

As his chest heaved from breathing hard, like I'd knocked all the oxygen out of his lungs, he walked backward out of the room. Not knowing how I was going to make it through another day on assignment with him, I hurriedly locked the door and threw on a pair of shorts and a tank top. After that, I headed out of the bedroom and then out the front door. Not long after, I was standing right by the swelling tide of the ocean. The waves pushed cool water toward my feet, instantly changing my foul mood. How dare Miles try to force himself on me! I'd told his ass no, and I hadn't given him mixed messages. His declaration of love further proved that crime in Jamaica wasn't all that I had to worry about. He'd made it off his rocker, and I was worried that he would drop the ball on the investigation.

Looking down at my cell phone, I wanted to call Special Agent Morris to let him know that I wanted off the case. Miles was a loose cannon, and I didn't want to take any chances. Then again, I also didn't want to risk the promotion that was looming in my future. *Damn*. What was I going to do? As I strolled along the beach, I hoped that putting that gun in Miles's face had shown him that I was serious as hell. If he tried it again, I'd surely do whatever I had to do, but until then, I'd just play it by ear. It wasn't like he was really a rapist. I guessed he thought I'd give in eventually, but my actions had shown him that I wouldn't.

Why did men think they could just violate a woman like that? Whether I'd fucked him before or not didn't give him a right to do what I had told him not to. Tears burned my eyes as I thought about all that I was sacrificing. I did have feelings for Miles, but he'd told me time and again that leaving his wife was out of the question. Being a mistress wasn't something that I'd envisioned for myself, and I wasn't about to take that title now. If I was going to have a man, I wanted him to claim me as his own. Sharing a man with his wife wasn't something I wanted.

The sound of my phone ringing in my hand made me look down at the screen. It wasn't a number I recognized, but I answered, anyway.

"Hello?"

"Indica, dis is Gaza. Is dis a bad time?"

"Oh, no, not at all. Me and Sway were just wrapping up our business and heading home."

"Cool. Mi want to link up with you tomorrow so we can talk more about what we talked about earlier."

"Umm . . . okay. What time do you want to meet up with us?"

"No, just you. I don't want your brother to come. I think we should keep this between us. Is that irie?"

"I guess, but I don't have a car. Sway does, but—"

"No worries. I'll pick you up. Just shoot me the address, and I'll be there tomorrow, around two p.m. That cool?"

"Yes, it is. I'll see you soon."

My heart skipped a beat as I ended the call. It kind of rubbed me the wrong way that he wanted to meet me without Miles, but I needed to get away from "my brother." Maybe, just maybe, I'd crack the case myself and leave Miles to wallow in his hurt feelings.

The next day I was up by 6:00 a.m., anxious to meet with Gaza. Most of the first half of my day was spent outside, by the pool. I ate a light breakfast of scrambled eggs, toast, sausage, and coffee alone by the pool and didn't bother to cook anything for Miles. After that shit he'd pulled the night before, I didn't know if I ever wanted to be near his ass again. Was he really capable of rape? Shit, I couldn't call it. All I knew was, he'd violated me for the first and last time. After writing an update report for Special Agent Morris, I decided to take a dip in the pool. Once I was done with my swim, I headed upstairs to get dressed for my meeting with Gaza.

When I stepped into the sitting room, fully dressed, Miles looked up at me, and his eyes widened. "Where are you going?"

"I have a meeting with Gaza. He's going to put me in on his money scam."

"You're going by yourself?"

"Technically. Look, don't start with that jealous bullshit. This is all business. I need you to access the GPS system and hack into his phone's mic and camera. Record everything he says, and when you get the location, make sure you do surveillance from a distance, just in case something happens. You know he and his crew are hot around here by what happened at the club the other night."

"I'm on it, but for some reason, I feel like you're trying to do some solo shit." Miles was shirtless, in only his pajama pants. He probably thought his broad chest was enticing me, but I was repulsed by him.

"Well, I advise you to get out of your feelings. We need to close this case as soon as we can, because I don't think I can stay here with you much longer. After the shit you did last night . . ."

"I'm sorry about that. That's not me, and you know it. There's just something about you that does something unexplainable to me. I act on impulse, when I'm normally more . . . rational.

Don't worry. It'll never happen again. I get the point. You don't want to fuck with me like that, and I respect that. Besides, I probably had one drink too many."

His apology sounded sincere, so I relented and accepted; however, I would still be on guard around him.

"Okay, apology accepted, but if you ever touch me again, you'll pay for that shit."

"I got you." He looked down at the laptop on the table in front of him, as if to say the conversation about that was over.

My phone rang. It was Gaza, so I figured he had arrived to pick me up. I picked up.

"Gaza, did you find the place okay?"

Miles glanced up at me with a smirk on his face as he shook his head.

"Yeah. Mi outside now."

"Okay. I'll be right out."

"I'm accessing Gaza's phone now, so I'll be on my way a few minutes after you leave," Miles assured me.

Nodding at him, I headed to the front door. "All right. Keep your head in the game, Miles."

When I got in the black Mercedes-Benz with Gaza, it smelled brand new.

"Nice ride," I complimented.

"Thanks. Mi just bought it this mornin'." His smile was radiant as his straight white teeth gleamed in the sunlight.

"Okay, you must be gettin' to that paper. Is this a twenty eighteen?"

"Hell yeah. It's fully loaded too. Dat's what comes with di territory, though. By di way, everything's been put in motion, so you'll have your keys soon." There was a contemplative look on his face as he drove.

"How soon is *soon*?"

"At least by tomorrow," he replied.

"A'ight. That's what's up. You're definitely right on time. I just got a call from my right-hand, and shit is gettin' low. I can't afford to fall off. Shit, I'm used to a certain lifestyle."

Gaza let out a light chuckle. "Mi feel yuh, beautiful."

The way he called me beautiful made my head spin and my body overheat. Or was it the fact that it was about a hundred degrees outside already? Nah, that couldn't be it, being that the air was on full blast.

The rest of the ride was in silence, and in less than forty minutes, we pulled up to a really nice condominium complex. Without saying a word, Gaza got out of the car and rushed around to my side to open my door. He put his hand out to take mine and helped me out of the car like a perfect gentleman.

"Is this your place?" I asked, surprised that he would bring me here.

"One of them," he told me as he led the way. "I don't really lay my head 'pon here that often, but it's a 'lay low' spot for me to chill and handle private meetings."

"Okay, so I take it that we will be the only two here."

"Yeah. I mean, is dat okay wit' you? I trust you enough to do business wit' you, so I'm sure you trust me enough to be alone wit' me."

"Oh, that's not a problem at all." Eyeing him flirtatiously, I added, "As a matter of fact, I prefer that."

"Yuh should, because my niggas was on yuh hard. All of dem was talkin' 'bout how you the perfect woman to have on their team. My nigga Royal said he like how you shot first and didn't ask any questions."

Once we were inside the cool building, I asked, "So, if you don't mind me asking questions now, what was that all about, anyway?"

We stepped into the elevator before he spoke. "Not too long ago, my nigga Gio was killed, and me and my niggas retaliated. After that shit, my girl got shot, and shit got even more real. We took care of the niggas who did that shit to her, and the cycle keeps going. Now these niggas want to keep comin' out like roaches. I won't stop till dey all dead and gone."

"So, Camille had already been shot before that dude put his gun to her head? Damn."

"Yup, once in the back, and a flesh wound to the leg. She's blessed to still be alive."

After we got off the elevator, I followed him, and we stopped at apartment 506. Gaza pulled out his keys, unlocked the door, and gestured for me to go inside. The place was decorated quite nicely for him never to be there. He walked in and led me to a brown butter-leather sofa.

"Take a seat. Would you like something to drink?"

"Yes. Some water please," I answered.

"Well, I was hoping you'd have a real drink with me. I got some good-ass Jamaican rum."

"Umm, no thanks." That man was too damn sexy for me to drink while we were alone. "I don't really drink like that, especially not this early."

"Yuh drank champagne last night."

"Well, that was only one glass. That was enough for the week." I let out a confident laugh. "I like to make sure I'm on point, especially when it comes to business."

"Mi overstand." He sauntered off to the kitchen and grabbed a bottled water for me. Then he grabbed the bottle of rum and a glass for himself.

After handing me the water and sitting down beside me, he placed the glass and the bottle of rum on the smoky glass coffee table and poured himself a shot. Then he pulled his cell phone from his pocket. "Mi gon' turn dis off, so mi can give you my undivided attention."

My heart stopped at the mention of him turning off his phone. Hopefully, Miles already had our location, but with Gaza's phone off, there would be no way for Miles to access his phone's camera and mic. *Shit!* It was a good thing I had a backup plan. My smart thinking had led me to consider that he'd be cautious; therefore, I had a tiny digital recorder clipped to my bra. The thing was, I was sure he wouldn't have me searched this time.

"Uh, yuh got your strap on you?" he asked me.

With a curt smile, I nodded. "Of course. I never leave home without it, but you don't have to worry. I won't shoot you."

He smiled back. "It's okay. Mi glad you kept your strap on you the other night. That shit kinda turned a nigga on." With a sly laugh, he put his phone down on the coffee table.

Although that statement got to me, I played it off. "Really now?"

Gaza grinned at me slyly. "Mi tink yuh should turn your phone off too."

Damn. So Miles wouldn't even be able to access my phone instead. "Why? I mean . . ."

"Just 'cause mi wan' your undivided attention too. What we are about to discuss is confidential. Mi would like it if yuh don't even share di details wit' your brethren."

"To be honest, Gaza, my brother's my partner. We have no secrets."

"Well, in dat case, mi guess we won't move any further with dis."

"Why? It's not like he's going to tell anyone. I mean, damn, he's about to buy a hundred kilos from you."

"And that's that, but mi don' want him in on dis shit. Mi just need an American woman's voice for dem to hear on di other line. For some reason, Americans trust other Americans, which is dumb as fuck. When dey hear a foreign accent, dey automatically hang up, tinkin' it's a scam."

"Well, it is," I added for good measure.

"Which is the reason I need yuh on my team. Yuh feel me, star? Yuh can make millions."

"Yeah, and I won't tell Miles anything about this."

After he took a shot of liquor, Gaza's eyes met mine in a lustful gaze. "So, he don't know yuh wit' me right now?"

"No. I told him I had called a driver and was going to do some shopping."

"Good," he remarked and poured himself another shot.

As I sipped my water, I waited for him to get down to business. Not long after, he did. In less than an hour I knew everything I needed to know about the scam he was in on. He wanted me to be the one who conducted the correspondence with potential victims in the United States. That shit was perfect, Everything that he had said was recorded and sent straight to the federal database. The evidence against Gaza and his crew was adding up, and I couldn't help but wear a satisfied, shit-eating grin on my face.

A few hours later, Gaza stood and told me that he was taking me home. Everything had been professional, and he'd fed me a hearty lunch too. We'd had curry goat, roti, steamed rice, and cabbage.

"That food was yummy," I told him as he led me to the door.

"Thanks to my favorite cook." He smiled. "Amya is my cousin and my personal chef. She cooked everything and left before you got here."

"Well, let her know that it was the best food I've ever tasted in my life."

"Mi sure will."

We made it to his car, climbed in, and headed toward the villa. All I could do was hope the case ended soon, because there was no way I could be left alone with Gaza on a regular basis. The sexual tension was thick enough to cut with a knife. We made small talk as he lit a blunt and offered it to me. After refusing, I had to smooth it over.

"No, like I said, I had enough weed and drink for the week."

"Let mi find out you ain't really a gangsta," he teased.

"I'm a hustler, and my money comes before pleasure," I told him, making it clear that I wasn't one who'd put pleasure before my funds. "I secure the bag, and *then* I enjoy myself."

"Smart thinking, and that's why mi wants to fuck wit' yuh. Hmm . . ." He looked over at me and licked his thick, sexy lips. "More mu'fuckas need to tink like yuh."

When I got back to the villa, I realized that Miles wasn't there. He must've been on his way back. I decided to get comfortable and wind down a little bit, so I took a seat on the sofa and leaned back. Playing the part of Indica was exhausting, so it felt good to be myself. Less than twenty minutes later, Miles walked in, seemingly in a foul mood.

"What the hell is wrong with you?" I scolded.

"So, you both turned your phones off," he spat.

"You know he's being cautious. Besides, I had a plan B, so everything he said was recorded and stored in the FBI database. I already alerted Special Agent Morris. It's no big deal."

"You're really being naïve and oblivious to what kind of man Gaza is. Do you realize that you were with a very dangerous man, with no backup? It's a good thing I had enough sense to follow you two right away, so I was able to watch your location. Be careful, Cathy."

Miles walked off in a huff, and I sat there wishing he'd just let me do things the way I saw fit. From where I was standing, I was making more progress with Gaza than he was. Maybe he was jealous because I was getting somewhere with the case in such a small amount of time, and because he thought Gaza was into me. What he didn't need to do was worry about me.

"I'm a big girl. I don't need you to protect me. We both know that," I threw over my shoulder with an attitude, though I wasn't sure if he was within earshot.

Letting out a deep sigh, I closed my eyes and massaged my temples. I couldn't wait for this shit to be over with. We'd been in Jamaica for only two days, and I was ready to go. It was a different story to be here due under these circumstances. It damn sure wasn't a vacation. While I sat there musing, my phone vibrated, and I looked down at the screen. It was Gaza, so I picked up.

"We'll be making the exchange tomorrow, around six. I'll let you know where to meet at before then," he said, his deep voice penetrating my eardrums.

"Damn, you're on it."

"Gotta be. Time is money. Until next time. Take care, Indica."

"You too, Gaza."

Chapter Twenty

Catherine

A month later . . .

Still in Jamaica, building our case against Gaza, Miles and I were talking less and less by the day. The only time we conversed was when we absolutely had to. I was also getting a little homesick, and I longed for my own personal space, instead of being in the middle of paradise with someone who seemed like a stranger to me. At this point we had enough evidence to lock up Gaza and his entire crew for the rest of their natural lives. The number of bodies on their hands was possibly enough for them to get the death penalty, given that some of the murders they were connected to had occurred in the United States.

Over time we'd done more than one drug transaction with Gaza. Of course, we'd gotten

the hundred keys and he'd gotten his money, but
Gaza hadn't been physically involved in the transaction. We could get him for conspiracy, though,
because I had the recording of us hashing out the
details. Not long after that, we had got about fifty
pounds of ganja from him. I had collected all the
information I needed about the ganja farm that
he got that shit from. In addition, I'd infiltrated
the scam he was involved in. Gaza and I had been
spending more time together without Miles, and
it was clear that he'd accepted me as part of his
crime syndicate. That shit was all falling into
place, and only a few loose ends had to be tied
before an arrest could be made.

The drugs had all been shipped to the United
States, where the Feds had eventually picked
them up by posing as undercover drug mules.
The coke and the marijuana would be housed
in the evidence room in the federal building
until the arrests and trials took place. The government funds that had been used to purchase
the drugs would be recouped after Gaza and his
men were charged with their crimes and were
behind bars. All their houses, cars, cash, and
other assets would be seized and later sold in
government auctions. That money would go
back to the government to stop more bad guys,

as well as into the bank accounts of some of the higher ranked federal agents.

Miles was feeling some type of way because Gaza never included him in anything other than the drug transactions. He was never really invited to any parties or get-togethers that Gaza had. I was always invited, though, and the last time, I'd decided to bring Miles along to clear the air. He had to understand that it wasn't personal. Like Gaza had said, he just needed a street-smart chick on his team. There were plenty of niggas around him just like Miles, so he had no real need for him other than what he thought was his money.

"So, you brought your brother, huh?" Gaza had asked when he had the chance to talk to me without ears around.

"Well, he's overprotective, Gaza. He's not that comfortable with us possibly doing business without him. I haven't told him anything."

"Or is he worried about something else happening between us?" Gaza's eyes had sparkled menacingly as he held a champagne flute up to his full lips and took a swig.

"That's not possible. He knows me. I don't mix business with pleasure."

Gaza offered me a glass of champagne. "Mi know yuh don't drink like dat, but make an exception for me. We have to celebrate. Since you came in on dis shit mi been building, mi 'ave made over twenty million in a month. Dat's worth toasting to."

After taking the glass from him, I held it up and clinked it against his. "I'll drink to that." As I turned the glass up, I looked around at the large crowd of partygoers. "It seems like you all just find any excuse to celebrate. In one month alone, I've been to at least five of these functions."

"Well, expect to celebrate some more. Part of di culture is to celebrate life. As a matter of fact, mi 'ave tis ting tomorrow. Mi need a beautiful woman to accompany me. Mi hope you're free." His eyes sparkled as he looked down at me.

"Shouldn't you take your girl?"

My question made him laugh good-naturedly. "To be one hundred wit' yuh, mi don' know if she even wanna be my girl anymore. Her mom's been gettin' in her head 'bout me. Since dat episode at di club, it's been tension, yuh know? She even packed a bag and left the other night. She claim my lifestyle's too dangerous for her, and she left the Gully to stay outta bullshit. Mi told her she can go if she like. Mi guess mi single now."

"Really?" After giving him a skeptical smirk, I looked away quickly. "Well, maybe she just needs some space. That doesn't mean your relationship is over. I don't mind accompanying you, but it'll be as a business associate. Nothing more, nothing less."

"Irie, mi guess dat's good enough." With a smile, he kept his eyes on me, making me kind of nervous.

I returned his smile and turned to walk away. I figured it was time to leave.

"Where yuh goin'?" His voice broke through my resistance.

"Home. It's getting late and . . ."

"You're a grown-ass woman. Don't leave just yet. I'm really enjoyin' your company."

After turning on my heels to face him, I shook my head at him. "Is that because you're having problems with your lady?"

"Nah, it's because mi really actually enjoy your company. If your brother wants to leave, that's fine. I'll be happy to take yuh home."

His expression showed that he really meant it, but what was he up to? *Damn.* Maybe Miles was right. The way he looked at me was intense, and I could feel that shit all in my bones. So it was best for me to take Gaza in small doses.

"I really have to go. I'll see you tomorrow . . . ?"

"I'll pick you up by eight. Be dressed to impress."

"Will do," I told him before putting my empty champagne glass on the bar.

I spotted Miles and walked over to him. "Are you ready to go, bro?"

Flashing a slick smile in my direction, he cleared his throat. "Nah, actually, I think I want to stay a little bit longer."

I followed his eyes as he stared at some thick, dark-skinned chick who was practically naked. She kept on grinding and winding her waist, and every man in the room was staring. Obviously, he'd spotted some pum pum.

"Well, I'm ready to go," I told him. "Give me the car keys. I'm sure you'll find a way back to the spot."

With his eyes still glued on ole girl, he passed me the car keys with no hesitation. "You're right. I'll get back there. Be safe."

He walked off and stood behind the chick he'd been gawking at. As he slow ground into her ass, I left the party, wondering exactly how shit was going to go down with Gaza the next day. The attraction between us was getting stronger, and as much as I tried to ignore our chemistry, that shit wasn't easy at all. The way I saw it, if Special Agent Morris didn't pull the plug on this operation soon, I'd be doing some things that would not be approved by the FBI.

***

The next morning, I noticed that Miles still hadn't returned to the villa. The only reason I knew this was that his bedroom door was wide open, his bed was made, and he was nowhere to be found. The day went by quickly, and by 6:00 p.m., Miles still hadn't returned. I called his phone because I was concerned about him. We were in Jamaica, and I didn't know if he'd been hurt or killed. Besides, that chick who kept dancing all freaky like may have had a nigga who was up in there. What if he'd slit Miles's throat with a machete or something? All types of thoughts went through my mind as his phone rang.

"Yeah?" he finally answered, as if I was bothering him.

"Uh, I take it that you're alive."

"Why wouldn't I be?"

"Well, if you must know, anything can happen. You could have at least called or texted me to let me know that you were okay," I scolded.

"Oh, so who's jealous now?"

"Boy, bye. That's far from what it is. You are my partner, and we are involved in some shady shit. In case you haven't noticed, we're in hostile territory. I was just worried about you, but since you're okay, continue doing what you're doing."

"And I will. Don't wait up." He hung up the phone, and I shook my head as I hung up. All I could do was hope he'd be safe.

Soon it was time for me to get dressed for the function I was attending with Gaza tonight. I took a shower, dried off, and then put on a tight black bandage dress that hugged every curve of my body like a glove. I slipped my feet into a pair of heels, and as a finishing touch, I dabbed on some tantalizing perfume.

Half an hour later, Gaza called me to let me know that he was outside. My plan was to seal the deal and get Gaza to admit to actually putting in motion some of the murders that had happened in the United States. He had admitted to some murders in Jamaica, but that wouldn't help our case. If he had put out hits on people in the United States, that would really drive the nail into his coffin. Hopefully, the tight-ass dress I was wearing and my sweet perfume would enable me to coax more information out of him. *Shit*. I wished I could get my hands on some type of truth serum, but I was sure that if he had enough drinks, he'd be singing like a canary.

This time I wasn't wearing a digital voice recorder, but I'd already accessed his phone's mic and camera for recording. More than likely, he'd keep his phone on, because he trusted me now. Soon I'd be leaving Jamaica and returning to my life and the promotion I'd worked so hard for. Damn. I couldn't wait.

When we arrived at our destination, Gaza jumped out, opened the car door for me, and grabbed my hand. Always the gentleman, he looped his arm through mine before we walked toward a large yacht that was docked at the pier. The sunset was beautiful, with its pink and purple shades sweeping across the sky. The thing was, I didn't see any other cars parked by the pier. Were we early? As I looked up at him, it was as if he'd read my mind.

"It's just us once again, but no matter what yuh say, this isn't just business," he remarked.

His fine ass had me swooning, but one thought came to mind. I'd heard all about how Jamaican men were players who prided themselves on having more than one woman at their disposal.

Pulling away from him, I tried not to seem rude, but I had to put my foot down. "But we both agreed that this would be about business, Gaza. C'mon, I've told you that over and over again . . ."

"Well, mi can't help but not believe you. I see the way you look at me. It's something between us, and mi don't wanna ignore it anymore. You can choose to, but the heart wants what the heart wants."

Did my heart really have anything to do with this situation, or was it just my pussy that seemed to jump whenever he was near me? I was caught between a rock and a hard place. I'd been playing with fire. I'd taken Special Agent Morris's words way too lightly, and it was as if I'd invited the extra attention that Gaza was showering me with. My superior had told me to do whatever I needed to do to get to Gaza, and I had, but maybe I'd gotten caught up in the process.

"Are you speaking about my heart or yours?" I returned. "Because I don't have those types of feelings."

"Once again, mi don't believe you. You're good at keeping yourself guarded. You're hard, to a certain extent, but, baby girl, you feel so soft." His fingers glided across my shoulder as we ascended the steps to the yacht.

"No, really, like I said before, I'm all about my money, Gaza," I insisted once we reached the starboard deck and came to a stop. "Any time that we've spent together, I've enjoyed, but I know better than to get involved with someone I make money with. Besides, Camille is in love with you, and I'll be returning to the States soon. I've had enough drama in my life, and I don't need any more. All I wanted was to help my brother find a connect and seal the deal. We did that. You wanted me in on a moneymaking situation, and I fulfilled that. We made money, and now I'm done. My life in the United States goes on . . ."

"Without me?" He raised my chin with his hand, making me look into his eyes, which were pulling me in.

"What do you mean? We will continue to buy from you." I let out a confident laugh, but I wasn't really feeling in control at all. If anything, I felt more vulnerable than ever.

"Mi not talkin' 'bout dat. Look, I can tell I'm making you uncomfortable. You've been in a man's world so long, you seem to have hardened yourself. I can see right through that shell, though. I know how it is. You must protect yourself, but I won't hurt you. No matter what happens from this point on, I just want whatever is brewing between us to flow. Just let it. If you go back to the United States, that's fine. I just don't want to live with one regret when it comes to you."

His lips were so close to mine, I could feel his warm, minty breath on my skin. Moving away a mere half an inch, I stopped the kiss before it could even happen. "Why are we here?"

"I'll slow down a little. We're going to have a nice dinner on the water, and then we're going to dance the night away. All I want is to spend some time with you that has nothing to do with business. Then you can see for yourself that this is a reason we met. It wasn't just to move kilos. I can bet my life on that."

My heart sank. If only he knew. Gaza was definitely what the natives called a gallist, but there was something that was still genuine about him. He had a way of looking at life that was refreshing. It didn't really matter to me if he was a drug dealer, a murderer, or a scam artist. . . . There was still something so alluring and intriguing about his humanity. Although he did bad shit, he didn't seem malicious at all. It just seemed that he did what he felt he had to do to survive, even if it was by illegal means. Everything I felt about him contradicted everything I'd learned during my training.

We headed to the large flybridge and sat down at a beautifully decorated round table with a lacy white tablecloth, fancy china, white orchids, and fragrant white candles. Once we were seated, the server brought out our dinner of steamed red snapper stuffed with okra, white rice, and

Jamaican water crackers. There was a fancy bottle of Chardonnay on ice, and the server filled our glasses.

"Can I have water with lemon please?" I asked.

"Of course," the server said and then walked away.

Gaza snickered. "You just can't let go, can you?" Shaking his head, he squirted lemon juice on his fish.

I did the same with my fish. "I just don't know how to take this. Tonight went from me escorting you to a function to me being your date. I wasn't prepared for this."

"Be spontaneous, beautiful. Life is about more than money and crime. You seem so preoccupied with that. I'd love to see you let go and let your hair down. You're far too beautiful to take life so damn seriously. Loosen up and live a little."

"It's not that easy for me. Being a woman in a male-dominated business, I have to always be on my shit," I said as the server placed a glass of water adorned with a lemon slice in front of me and then disappeared again. "If I ever slip up and involve my heart, it could cost me my life. We both know that. There is some type of chemistry between us, but I think it's only to make money together. Don't read too much into it. You're an attractive man—don't get me wrong—but it's nothing more than that between us, Gaza. You're better off with Camille. She balances you out, whereas I'd just add more chaos to your life."

"I like chaos. Every man likes a challenge, and you're challenging me." I liked how he'd adjust his language for me and abandon the patois. His accent was still strong and sexy, though.

"You may think you want to go there, but I assure you, you don't, Gaza. Let's just leave it where it is. Okay . . . ?"

The food was delicious, but my appetite had waned a little due to the fact that the inevitable seemed to be happening. Who was I fooling? I was feeling Gaza just as much as he was feeling me, if not more, but I had so much to lose.

"Okay," he agreed, finally backing off. "I'm sorry if I'm coming on too strong. It's just, well . . . I know what I want, and I go after it. It's the ambition in me."

"Well, I'm a woman, not a goal."

"Oh, believe me, you're a goal, a gorgeous one at that." After taking a sip of wine, he licked his enticing lips.

That made me blush against my will.

"It's okay to let go, Indica. You can with me. Just let whatever is meant to happen, happen. Are you enjoying your food?"

"Yes, it's really good." Using my fork to move the food around on the plate, I tried to force myself to eat.

"Am I making you nervous?"

"No, I just, uh . . ." Before I could get the words out, his lips were on mine, capturing what I didn't have the chance to say.

Instead of pulling away, I went in. Damn, his tongue was so sweet, and his lips were so warm and soft. I found myself moaning. Next thing I knew, we were both on our feet without breaking our kiss. Gaza's arms were around my waist, and then he was leading me away from the table. Soon we were belowdecks, where there was an extravagant master stateroom with low, romantic lighting. There were rose petals leading to the bed, and on the self-service bar was another bucket of ice with a bottle of wine.

Before I could talk some sense into myself, I just did what he said and let go. Without using my head, I let my body take over, which had been a reoccurring mistake of mine. Often I found myself letting my pussy think for me. The wetness that dripped onto my panties was something I just couldn't defy. At that moment, I was weak, and as I turned into putty in Gaza's hands, I didn't think about the consequences.

"Just let go, baby. Let me make you feel good," he said as we stood in the center of the stateroom. With his hands caressing my skin, he slowly removed my dress and then my underwear. "Mmm . . ." He stood back to admire my naked frame. "Keep those heels on. Damn, you thick as fuck . . ."

The next instant, his mouth was on my breasts, and he sucked on each of my nipples ever so gently as his hands continued to explore. As he cupped my ass cheeks, he let out a deep sigh. Me, on the other hand, I was in pre-orgasmic heaven. Something told me that I was about to have some of the best dick of my life, and my skin became feverish from lust. Nobody had to know we fucked, regardless of how things turned out. Even if he said that we had, I'd just deny that shit. As far as I was concerned, I just needed to release all the tension that had built up inside me. *Damn it.* A bitch needed to cum.

After he laid me down on the bed, Gaza's warm, wet tongue glided along my anatomy, causing me to writhe with pleasure.

"Mmm . . . ohhh . . . ," I moaned as he sucked on my clit like an expert.

Doing all types of tongue tricks, he slurped and sucked, causing me to grab the back of his head. My thighs clenched his face in a vise grip.

A tingling feeling took over me as I bucked and ground my pussy, anticipating the nut that he would so graciously bestow upon me. He stared into my eyes as he witnessed the control that he had over me at that moment. Seeing the pleasure that he got out of pleasing me, I was ready to return the favor. Then it occurred to me that he wasn't and would never be my man, so I fought the urge to pull his dick out and deep throat that shit. I'd seen his thick-ass print in his pants and knew that he was working with something.

Undressing slowly, he threw his clothes to the side as I watched attentively. Then he lay down next to me, and as I ran my hands over his pecs and six-pack abs, I could feel the moisture still pouring from me. He had me wet as hell, which was a good thing, given that he was working with a monster. That nigga's dick looked like an elephant trunk, but for some reason, I felt like I could take that shit. He climbed on top of me, and his tongue ignited the flesh on my neck. Suddenly, he stopped kissing on me, picked up a gold-foil wrapper on the nightstand, then tore it open to release the condom. Sliding it down the shaft of his engorged dick, he continued to stare at me with longing.

He leaned over, and his lips met mine again as he parted my thighs with his strong hands. Feeling his hardness making its way inside my wet tightness, I held my breath and raked my nails softly across his back. Damn, his long, thick-ass dick had my pussy wide the fuck open. As he slid against my sugar walls, he found the way to my spot way too fast. Moving his body on top of me like a serpent, he worked his back and ass, grinding all nasty like. The sound of my wetness mixed with my moans, making the moment way too damn erotic.

"Shit! Damn, Gaza!" I heard myself scream out as I held on to him for dear life.

My legs were wrapped around his waist as he groaned his ecstasy into my ear. "Fuck, Indica . . . Yo' pussy's way too tight, star. Jah know this pussy's too fuckin' good. Mmm . . . uhhh . . . work it, Mami. Work that pum pum on dis wood. Bruk that shit off, Mama. Fuck, yeah . . . arghhh . . ."

His eyes rolled back, and he bit down on his bottom lip as he flipped me over so that he could hit it from the back. The sound of him slapping my ass cheeks and the gushiness of my depths were the soundtrack for our fuck session. We didn't need any music or nothing else to get us in the mood. The two of us were just like two magnets attracting each other, because it was just nature.

"I'm 'bout to cum. Shit!" I exclaimed, then let out a squeal. The back shots that Gaza was putting down on me had me so fucked up. My left leg shook, and pussy juice squirted out of me like a geyser as I came harder than I ever had. "Ohhh . . . uhhh . . . damn . . ." My eyes rolled back in my head, and that nigga kept right on thrusting and holding on to me for dear life.

His dick seemed to be growing inside of me, and then I felt it start to throb inside of me. That was a clear sign that he couldn't take how my pussy muscles were contracting and massaging his shit. He stared deeply into my eyes and his hands held on tightly to my waist as his mouth fell wide open.

"Arghhh . . . shit . . . Dis bloodclat pussy fye!"

Quickly, he pulled out of me and went to flush the condom in the toilet of the en suite bathroom. Then I heard the water running. When he returned to the stateroom, he had a warm cloth to wash me off with. After he washed me off, he joined me in the bed and assumed the spooning position. Both of our breathing was still labored, and we said nothing as we calmed down from the moment.

"I'll kill for you. Mi just want you to know that," he whispered in my ear.

"How can you do that if I'm going to the United States soon?"

"Hmm . . . I can touch niggas in the United States. That ain't shit for me. Where I can't go, I got mu'fuckas ready to do whatever the fuck I want. Shit. It's been done before."

"So you've put hits out on niggas in the States?"

"Hell yeah. Plenty of times. And I'll do it again if I have to. I ain't go nowhere."

"You're a powerful man, Gaza . . ."

"And you're a powerful woman, Indica. Damn, mi knew dat pum pum was gon' be good as fuck. Got me all into you even more now. We could be a real power couple, simi?"

"What could be and what will be are totally different, Gaza. You know this shit is complicated. You haven't handled your situation with Camille, and I'll be going back to New York soon . . . I let shit flow, but we can't be together."

He kissed my forehead softly. "Mi know dat. Just promise me dis won't be the last time I get to feel you."

"I can't . . ."

"Fair enough fi me. How 'bout you just let me hold you for a li'l while? Can you do that?"

Against my better judgment, I agreed. Besides, I had ridden there with him. Honestly, I was spent, so in no time I was fast asleep in his arms.

***

The midmorning sun peeked through the window of the yacht's master stateroom, waking me from my good post-sex slumber. The sight of Gaza's handsome face reminded me of the forbidden act we'd indulged in the previous night. Suddenly, reality sank in, and I was sober. What the fuck was I thinking? Gaza was snoring lightly, and I woke him up to let him know that I needed to go.

"Okay," he sighed and sat up, with a groggy look on his face. "I need some coffee. Damn, you're even beautiful first thing in the morning. Mmm . . ." He caressed my cheek before standing up and leaving the stateroom.

Soon he returned with a mug of coffee for me.

"Thanks," I told him, not knowing what else to say. Once again, I'd ended up in bed with the wrong man, and once again, that shit could cost my career.

"Get dressed. There's breakfast waiting for us. After you're nice and full, I'll get you home, beautiful." The next second his lips were on mine, and I couldn't help but wonder what would happen if he knew the truth. To be for real about it, if I wasn't who I was, and I was really Indica, I could see myself with him.

The ride back to the villa wasn't laced with much conversation. I figured we were both contemplating the intensity of what had happened and what we were going to do about it. One thing I knew was we couldn't continue to fuck around if I had to stay there longer. There was a moment when the line had to be drawn in the sand, and it was now.

"Look, Gaza, last night was incredible, but it can't happen again." He had just stopped right in front of the villa, and I had to cut shit off before it got out of hand.

Gaza turned to me and grabbed my hands. "Last night was more than incredible. I respect whatever yuh want to do, but mi won't pretend dat it's nothing happening here, Indica. You feel it too, but I'll give you the time to admit it."

Before I stepped out of the car, we shared one last sweet kiss.

My head was swimming when I used my key in the door and walked inside the villa. What I didn't expect was to find Miles sitting there on the sofa with a scowl on his face.

"Are you fucking crazy, Cathy! You fucked him!"

"What?" Giving him a shocked look, I pretended that he was out of his mind.

"Don't play dumb with me. I accessed your location by GPS and hacked into your phone's mic and camera. Not only did I watch you get on that yacht with Gaza, but I heard everything. I even saw some of it, before y'all moved away from the camera. You're in too deep, Cathy, and I've already let Special Agent Morris know what's going on."

"You didn't dare!"

"Yes I did, and we are going back to the States tomorrow. There was no reason for you to fuck him, other than the fact that you wanted to! I knew it! And you possibly fucked up your promotion because you let that goon get the pussy you won't let me have."

"So, that's what this is all about! You are mad because I fucked Gaza and won't fuck you. Must I remind you that I did all the work here? All the shit we got on him is because of me. So what if I fucked him? If a female was the person we were investigating and *you* fucked her, nobody would think anything of it. I got my rocks off, and damn, it was good as hell. He fucked me better than you ever could. I'll deal with Morris tomorrow. As far as you, when we back to New York, I want you to leave me the fuck alone."

"You might want to be careful what you wish for, because you might just find yourself left alone out in the cold with nothing. Once you fuck up with the Feds, you won't be getting another chance. Your pretty face and fat ass won't be able to help you when you can't get another job . . . You can kiss that promotion good-bye. I hope his dick was worth it."

"Fuck you, Miles, with your hating ass."

"You been involved in that street shit too long," he retorted. After turning his nose up at me, he got off the sofa and walked out of the room, leaving me there to think about the fact that one moment of bliss might have cost me my entire future.

Chapter Twenty-one

Catherine

The flight back to New York was long and tense. One thing I wasn't looking forward to was seeing Special Agent Morris when I got back. He'd already confirmed the warrant for Gaza's arrest and his extradition back to the United States to face charges. He hadn't reprimanded me over the phone, but he had told me to be in his office first thing Monday morning. Today was Sunday, and our flight would be landing at 5:30 p.m., so I didn't have much time to prepare my mind for what was going to happen tomorrow. Something told me that the promotion was off the table, but I prayed that I didn't lose the career I'd wanted all my life.

Of course, I didn't sit with that asshole Miles on the plane. He could've kept that shit between me and Gaza to himself. He'd spilled the beans only because he was jealous. After the plane landed, I rushed off to the baggage claim as I accessed my Uber app. The only thing I wanted to do was grab my shit and go the fuck home. Avoiding Miles was on my to-do list, but that shit wasn't going to happen. Before I knew it, he was right behind me.

"I told Morris only because I was worried about you getting in too deep with that shit. I think you got lost in the lure of Indica and your lust for Gaza. Cathy, I saw that shit coming, and you fell for it, anyway. You know what kind of man Gaza is, and you didn't have to fuck him to get what we needed for his arrest," he said over my shoulder.

"Okay, shit! I did it because I *wanted* to! Are you happy now! I didn't do it to get evidence. I did it because I wanted to fuck him! I wanted to know what it felt like to feel a powerful man inside me for once, since I always end up fucking bitch-ass, overgrown boys like you. I know what kind of man he is, but at least he's a man. I can't say the same for you. Now, leave me alone. You've done and said enough, Miles." Shaking my head, I grabbed my luggage off the carousel and walked briskly away. Hopefully, he wouldn't follow me this time. Without even looking back, I realized that he hadn't. *Good*. If I had the choice, I'd never see Miles's smug-ass face again.

The feeling of contentment and relief that engulfed my frazzled mind was welcome as I walked over the threshold of my condo. First thing, I jumped in the shower and washed all my stress away. When I got out, I dried off, put on some lotion, and slipped on a pair of boy shorts and a tank top. With furry slippers on my feet, I settled down in front of the TV and grabbed the phone. While ordering takeout from my favorite Chinese spot, I turned the television on. Before I could even finish placing my order, my phone beeped to let me know I had a call coming in. It was Anya's number. I hadn't spoken to her in about a week, so my plan was to check up on her after I ordered my food, but then I told myself to forget the food and to answer her call. I'd just have to call the restaurant back.

"Anya, boo . . . I've been meaning to call you, girl. I just got back—"

"This ain't Anya," a chilling voice literally growled into my ear.

"Tray?"

"Yeah. Your friends stopped watching the house and school a few days ago. I guess they thought I'd just back off, or they couldn't afford to put in the extra hours anymore. Whatever the case may be, I just want my family back. All you've ever done is interfere, and that shit stops today."

My breath caught as my heart rate increased. "Is Anya okay? Where are the twins?"

"I wouldn't hurt my wife and kids, Catherine. You obviously thought I would, or you wouldn't have had the cops watching my family like a hawk." He let out a sinister laugh.

"To be honest with you, I didn't think you would hurt them, but I was just being cautious. Just let me speak to Anya and the twins, so I'll know that they're okay."

"Nah. This call is only to let you know that Anya and the twins are going with me. We're leaving New York, and you'll never see them again. Don't you dare get your Fed friends or the NYPD involved, or I will hurt your best friend."

"Tray, no, please . . . Think about what you're doing. Anya's whole life is here, and the twins have their school and their friends. I won't involve the police, but I can't say that I won't find you."

"Find me, then, bitch." I was already trying to access Anya's phone's GPS on my laptop. Then I realized that Tray had hung up.

"Shit!" Dialing Anya's number, I prayed that he hadn't turned her phone off. It was a good thing that his phone number was still in the system. My next bet would be to access his phone's location.

Anya's phone continued to ring as I waited to get something. While the location of her phone was being searched on my laptop, I ran to my bedroom and threw on a pair of gray sweats and a T-shirt. By the time I had slipped on a pair of sneakers and grabbed my gun, there was a moving red dot on the laptop screen. His car was headed north, so I had to start following him ASAP. This time, I thought of calling for backup. I didn't have Anya to talk me out of that shit. Why hadn't Special Agent Morris told me that the NYPD had stopped watching her and the twins? I wondered. Maybe he didn't even know.

For some reason, I couldn't access the mic and camera on either of their phones. I left my condo with my laptop, then made my way to my car in the parking lot. After placing the laptop on the passenger seat, I climbed behind the wheel and took off. As I sped through the traffic, I kept glancing over at the laptop. But then the red dot on the screen disappeared. As if he knew how I'd found him the first time, he'd turned off both of their phones, and I now had no location. Something told me that it wouldn't be that easy to find Trayvon this time. I pulled over to the side of the road, picked up my phone, and called the NYPD. After letting the person who answered know that I was a federal agent, I explained the situation thoroughly.

"We do have that address logged for surveillance, but they stopped surveillance a couple of days ago. There is nothing here explaining why. I can definitely put out an APB for the vehicle, and I can contact local and surrounding authorities to be on the lookout for it."

"Please do that," I replied. "I know they are in danger. Can you tell the police to stay off his radar? He threatened to kill her and the kids if the police are involved."

Tears burned my eyes as I thought about what Anya and the twins could possibly be facing. The outcome didn't really seem promising this time, because even if he didn't hurt them, he planned to isolate them from everything they knew and loved. Wiping my tears away, I thought of calling Special Agent Morris, because he had more pull than I did. At this point, I didn't know what to do. As I rattled off the license-plate numbers for Trayvon's car and Anya's, which I'd written down on my phone, I wondered if my efforts were a little too late.

After going back home, because I didn't know where to search for my friend and my godchildren, I waited anxiously for some news. Instead of contacting Special Agent Morris, I decided to let the police take care of the situation. A few hours later I got an update from an officer with the NYPD. The authorities in the surrounding areas had been alerted and were looking for both vehicles I'd described, since I didn't know what Trayvon was driving. They also had physical descriptions of Trayvon, Anya, and the girls. The NYPD had searched Anya's home and had confirmed that no one was there and that there weren't any signs of foul play.

After that call ended, I paced my living room floor, I kept my eyes on my phone's screen, waiting for Anya to call to let me know that she was okay. When the phone finally rang, I anxiously waited to see my bestie's number, but Miles's number popped up instead. Rolling my eyes, I let out a frustrated sigh and sent him straight to voicemail. He called right back, and I sent him to voicemail again. When he called a third time, I huffed and decided to go ahead and answer.

"What the fuck do you want, Miles?"

"Well, damn. How are you?"

"Not too good right now. My best friend is in a very volatile situation with her estranged husband. I'm afraid he really lost it when he got the divorce papers that she had him served with. He called and told me that he was taking Anya and his twin girls away from here. I tried to trace his location, and I succeeded for a short while, but he's smart enough to know that I can

access his location through his cell phone. It's
either that or Anya broke down and told him. He
turned their phones off, so I'm home now, and
I don't know what the fuck to do. I got the cops
on it, and I'm hoping they find them alive. I'm so
scared he's going to do something crazy. I told
Anya that he was a ticking time bomb and that
she should have gotten him arrested when he
called himself kidnapping the twins." I was out
of breath by the time I finished, wondering why
I was even tell him all this. Miles had literally
ruined my life, but I didn't really have anybody
else to vent to.

"Shit. I'm coming over. You don't need to be
alone right now."

"No . . . don't . . . ," I told him quickly, but he'd
already hung up.

Although I didn't really want to see Miles, he
was right. I didn't need to be alone right now, but
did I want to be around him after what he'd done?
True, I'd fucked up by fucking Gaza, and I knew
that it looked bad. The thing was, it had been a
rebellious moment for me, but that wasn't how
I always was. Maybe I was too damn weak emo-
tionally to handle being an undercover federal
agent. The one chance I had had to prove myself,
and I had fucked the damn suspect. The fact was,
I hadn't been thinking. All my training and work

ethic had gone out the door because I had acted only on impulse. That was not a good look, and I was certain that I'd never get a promotion, based on my poor decision making. What if I was looked upon as a whore by Special Agent Morris? He'd possibly never trust me to conduct an undercover operation again. I'd gone against everything that I stood for, and for what? Shit, the dick was good, though.

My mind drifted back to Anya, and my eyes were once again glued to my phone's screen. Anya's number was in my head, and my prayers were that if it popped up on my phone again, it would be her voice I heard on the other end of the line. I prayed that the police would find them, apprehend Trayvon, and get Anya and the girls away alive and in one piece. That was all I wanted, and my tears began to fall again as I prayed out loud.

"Lord, I know that I'm nowhere near perfect, but my heart is good. That's probably my only downfall, and you know that. I love Anya, Kelsey, and Chelsey so much. Please keep them safe, because if something happens to them, I wouldn't know what to do. I wouldn't be able to handle it." My chest heaved as I tried to catch my breath. "Just keep them safe, Lord. In Jesus's name, I pray. Amen."

Right when I finished my prayer, the doorbell rang. After jumping out of my skin, because the sound scared me, I rushed to the door to look out the peephole. It was Miles, so I took in a deep breath before I opened the door. Before stepping over the threshold, he took me in his arms. The sobs really shook my body then. All I needed was someone to finally be there for me, even if it was a man I almost hated with all my heart.

Miles just held on to me, allowing me to let it all out. His hand softly caressed my back as he assured me that everything would be okay. "They will be fine. I contacted Special Agent Morris, and he has some of our best men on it."

"You tell him everything," I told him, pulling away from his embrace.

Miles closed the front door and followed me to the sofa. Taking my hand, he looked deeply into my eyes. "I didn't tell Special Agent Morris about you and Gaza. I was so mad, I just wanted to fuck with you. Once I realized what was going on, I stopped the recording. I'd never sabotage you like that. Morris was going to pull us off the case, anyway. At first, I was all in my feelings about you fucking him, but then I thought about it. I'm not the most righteous person in the world. We both know that. To be honest, if the shit was turned around and the person we were investigating was a sexy-ass female, there's no telling what I would've done. I'm hoping you get that promotion, because you did put in all the work." He paused for a moment. "I'm leaving my wife, Cathy. I'm sick of pretending that I love her when I don't. I realize that I can be a father without being her husband. Thank you for pointing that out for me when I should've been able to see it in the first place. I'm filing for a divorce in the morning."

"I'm grateful that you didn't rat me out to Morris, but why are you telling me about your divorce?"

He kissed my hand. "I actually admire you, and like I told you before, I fell for you. That's all on me, though. You told me from the jump that we couldn't have anything other than a physical relationship. I hoped for more, and when you didn't give me what I wanted, I acted like a spoiled-ass toddler. I'm sorry. I realize now that I flirt and have affairs because I'm not being fulfilled. I'm not with the right woman, and one day, I'm hoping I'll find that. Regardless of that, I want you to know that there's no animosity between us. We can still work together, and you don't have to worry about me crossing any invisible line that you draw. I just want us to remain friends, because I do care about you, Cathy. I know you slept with Gaza only because there's something missing in your life. It's the same thing that's missing in mine—true love. We all need someone to be there when we come home from a long, stressful day at work. I'm hoping we both find that . . . one day."

His words really touched me, and I couldn't help but hug him again. "Thank you, Miles. I'm hoping for the same thing, and I'm glad we were able to get to this point."

"Me too." He smiled at me and held me in his arms until I was finally able to fall into a restless sleep.

About an hour later, Miles woke me up.

"Wake up, Cathy. Your phone's ringing."

I jumped up and, embarrassed, wiped the slobber from the side of my mouth before I answered my phone. It was Special Agent Morris, and I prayed that he had some good news for me. It was after one in the morning, so I was hoping that they'd arrested Trayvon and that Anya and the girls were okay.

"Yes, Special Agent Morris?"

"Catherine, we found Trayvon Wheeler's car. Unfortunately, nobody inside it was alive. It looks like he killed his wife and his daughters and then himself. They all suffered from a fatal gunshot to the head."

His words registered, although it seemed like I couldn't hear him anymore. "Nooo!" I wailed, feeling my whole body grow weak just as Miles grabbed me. The guilt took over immediately as I dropped the phone on the floor. My tears were endless as Miles held on to me.

My best friend was all I had, and she and my goddaughters were gone. If only I could have done more. If only I'd gotten his ass arrested. Things would never be the same after that moment, and it felt like my world was spinning out of control.

"They're gone, Miles. All of them. That coward killed them, and he killed himself. He wasn't even man enough to deal with what he did. He took everything I loved away from me. If he wasn't dead, I'd kill him myself!" I wailed as Miles's arms tightened around my waist.

"I know, and I'm so sorry."

Unexpectedly, Miles was there for me when I needed him the most. Would I be able to keep going after such a loss? I didn't have a close relationship with my mother, and I had no siblings and no father. Anya and the girls were all I had, and now they were gone.

The next morning it took everything in me to get up and get dressed for work. Special

Agent Morris had given me the day off, but I had decided to go in, anyway. I'd take the time off for Anya's and the girls' funerals. Anya's mother was taking care of the arrangements and had assured me that she would keep me posted. What I needed at the moment was a distraction. When I got to the federal building, I headed straight to Special Agent Morris's office. He greeted me with a rare smile.

"I'm glad you made it, Agent Reed. I have great news for you, despite what you're going through. After this announcement, I really want you to take the day off. Well, that's after you go sign the paperwork for Gaza's arrest. They got him. He's already at the jail. Well, him and his organization. You did a great job, Reed. That's why you're being promoted." He passed me a badge with my name on it that gleamed in the light.

As much as I wanted that promotion, it was bittersweet. "Thank you, Special Agent Morris."

"No need to thank me. You did all the hard work."

I headed directly to the jail after I left my superior's office. Once I arrived there, I signed the paperwork for Gaza's and his men's arrest. It felt as if I was on autopilot as I exited the room where I had had to meet with the authorities that were taking over their custody. On my way out, I ran into Gaza, off all people, in shackles, handcuffs, and his state-issued khakis. A guard walked with him. He glared at me, with an evil smirk on his face, but didn't utter a word. Avoiding his eyes, I knew what he really wanted to say. At that point, he knew that I was a Fed and that I was the one who had brought down him and his crew. In his eyes, I saw the seed of vengeance being planted. What he didn't know was that I'd lost so much, just as he had. There was nothing I could do about it but live with the consequences.

One other thing that Gaza didn't know was . . . if I *really* were Indica, we'd be living in that mansion in the hills of Jamaica, taking over the world.

Chapter Twenty-two

Gaza

This was a night of celebration up in the mansion in Beverly Hills. The Big Man was so impressed by the amount of coke we moved and the money that was made, he had opened up his place for a night of partying. Bad bitches were everywhere: in the pool, in the house. It was a sight to see. The entire crew had been invited, which was a first, because up until now Leroy and I were the only ones he would meet face-to-face.

"Yo, Father, I'm glad you decide to do business wit' Indica and Sway," Leroy said as we sat across from each other, enjoying the breeze. "Look how much bloodclaat money we bring in over the last month or so. Jah know, star, I never know so much money was in coke until you and Gio show me how the thing set."

"Yo, only thing fucked is that Gio isn't here to celebrate with us. Jah know, star, I miss that nigga."

"You not the only one, Father. That nigga is missed. Everywhere I go, bitches and niggas always come up to me and tell me how much them miss Gio. Them bwoy deh take out a real youth for real, yo."

I nodded. "Big facts. But it's our night to celebrate, so let's kind of ease our mind a little."

"This where y'all niggas hiding out," Royal said as he stepped out onto the porch, where Leroy and I were sitting.

"What's good, nigga? I thought you was flying out tonight," I said.

"And miss this celebration? Hell nah. I see we young millionaires up in this bitch."

We exchanged daps, and he took a seat with Leroy and me. Something was bothering me, though. . . . Royal was supposed to be back in the States, so why was he here? I looked at him sitting there, chatting up a storm, but I felt that something was off. He seemed nervous. Like, he was talking, but he was not making any eye contact.

Maybe the alcohol was making me paranoid. I took a long pull out of my weed.

"So tell me, Royal, what's next, nigga?" I asked him.

Before I could get an answer . . .

"US marshals! Get down! Get down! Get down!"

I jumped up out of my seat and ran to the wall that enclosed the property. I climbed up, avoiding the barbed wire, and peered over. There had to be over a hundred SUVs and cars surrounding the property.

I jumped down, returned to the porch, and looked at Royal and then at Leroy. . . . Only one Judas was on that porch.

"You set me up, pussy?" I grabbed my Glock and poin-ted it at this nigga's dome.

"Gaza, no! I don't know what you talking 'bout, fam—"

Pop! Pop! Pop!

His body fell to the ground, blood splattering all over the white polo shirt that I had on. . . .

"I love you, my nigga," I said to Leroy. "We've been here before, in this same predicament, so we both know this is it for us—"

"Fuck that! I ain't going out like this," Leroy said as he ran to the door, waving a handgun.

"Put the fucking gun down," yelled a big white dude with a US marshal badge around his neck. He had a gun pointed dead at Leroy.

"Go suck you muma, white boy," Leroy said as he started squeezing the trigger. I watched as my nigga's body got riddled with bullets. I had to say that over thirty shots were fired into his body.

"Drop the fucking gun and get the fuck down, Donavan, aka Gaza," another dude yelled.

"We got the big fish, on the porch. We got Donavan!" shouted the big white dude who had shot Leroy.

Within seconds, around fifty marshals and police officers swarmed the porch.

I knew there wasn't no way out. I looked at the pussy nigga standing in front of me, smiled, and put the gun down. I then put my hands in the air. . . .

They quickly tackled me to the ground. One nigga put his foot in my back, as if I was resisting. I really wasn't.

They cuffed me and dragged me out. When we got outside, all my squad were also in cuffs, including the Big Man. He looked at me and shook his head.

I turned my head. What could I do? I did bring all this into his life, into my life. . . .

Camille was the only thing I could think about. . . .

Epilogue

Camille

I got up to use the bathroom, and when I came back into the bedroom, I realized Gaza hadn't made it home. I sat down on the edge of the bed, cut the light on, and grabbed my phone. It was well after 4:00 a.m. and the club was closed, so where the hell was the man? I had worked earlier, but I'd had a bad headache, so I'd come home early. The last time we spoke, it had been around 10:00 p.m. and he'd been in the car with Leroy. Matter of fact, he'd said they were on their way to a party. I hadn't asked where. Instead, I had told him that I loved him and then had hung up the phone. . . .

I grabbed the remote and cut the television on. There wasn't much on, until breaking news came on. . . . "Federal marshals, along with the Jamaica Defense Force, took down major drug kingpin Donavan, aka Gaza, hours ago."

The phone fell on the floor as I stood up and ran to the television.

"Nooo!" I screamed as I fell to the floor. "Oh, Lord, this can't be true . . ."

My head was spinning, and I couldn't breathe. I needed to think. I jumped out of the bed. I ran to the safe. *Think, Camille. Think* . . . Gaza had told me this code over and over again, just in case something like this were to happen.

After two failed tries, the safe popped open. My eyes popped open, too, as I had never seen so much fucking money in my life before. Not Jamaican dollars, but American dollars. I rushed back to the bedroom and grab a duffel bag that Gaza had in the closet. I rushed back to the safe and started throwing money in the duffel as fast as my hands would allow me.

I then dragged the heavy-ass bag into the kitchen and grabbed my car keys. Then I stepped into the garage and hit the button to open the garage door. . . .

"Get the fuck down, miss! Get down now!"

"God, please help me," I whispered as the tears started rolling down my face.

I dropped to my knees as they stormed into my life. . . .